THE DREAM HOUSE

and Other Stories

N. P. ARROWSMITH

DEACONSHIRE
TALES

Book Cover by Fay Lane

Map by Dewi Hargreaves

Chapter Heading Illustrations by Lindsay Baang

1st edition, 2025

To find out more about the author and to discover other books under the publishing entity, Deaconshire Tales, visit nparrowsmith.com

Joyce,
you still guide me

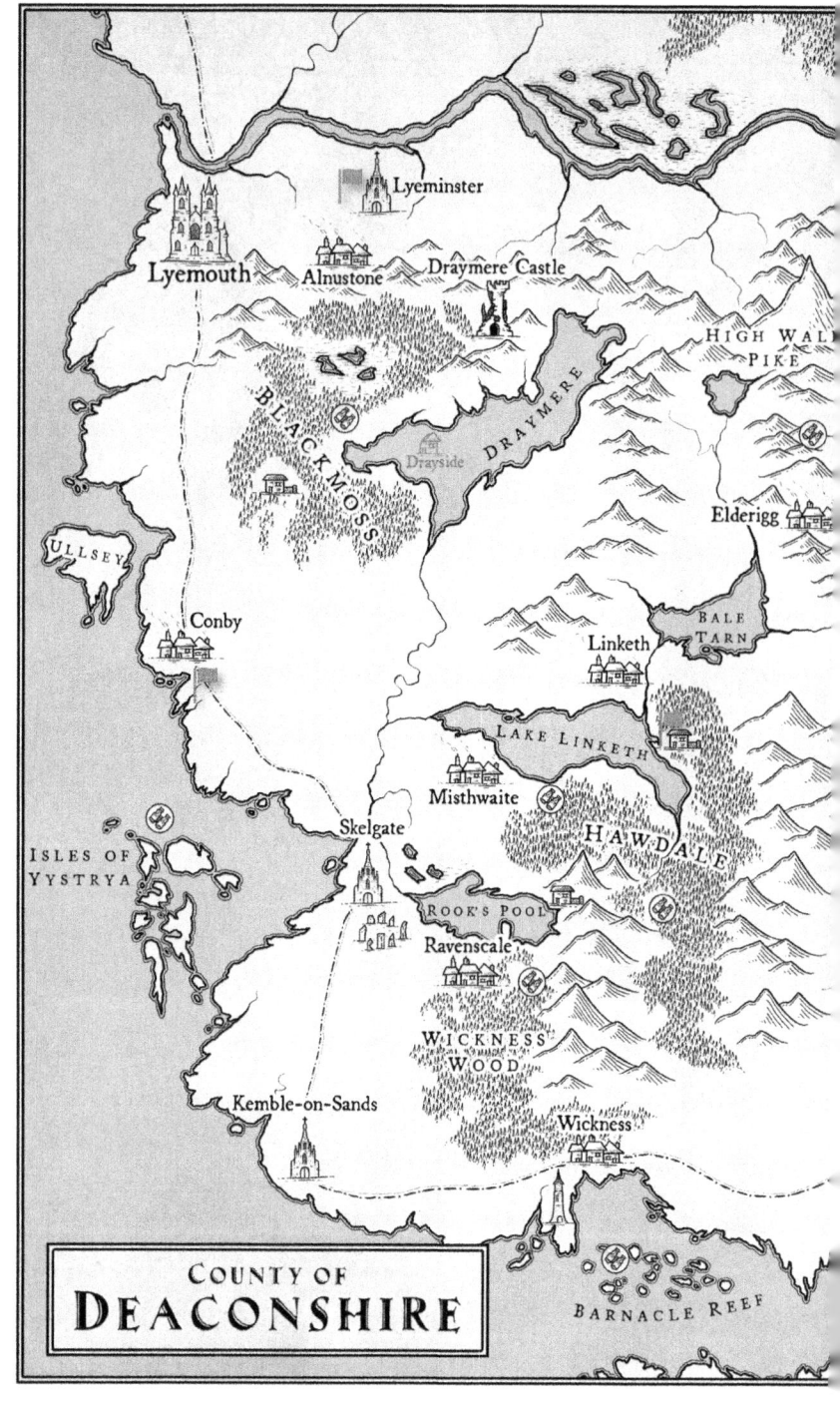

COUNTY OF
DEACONSHIRE

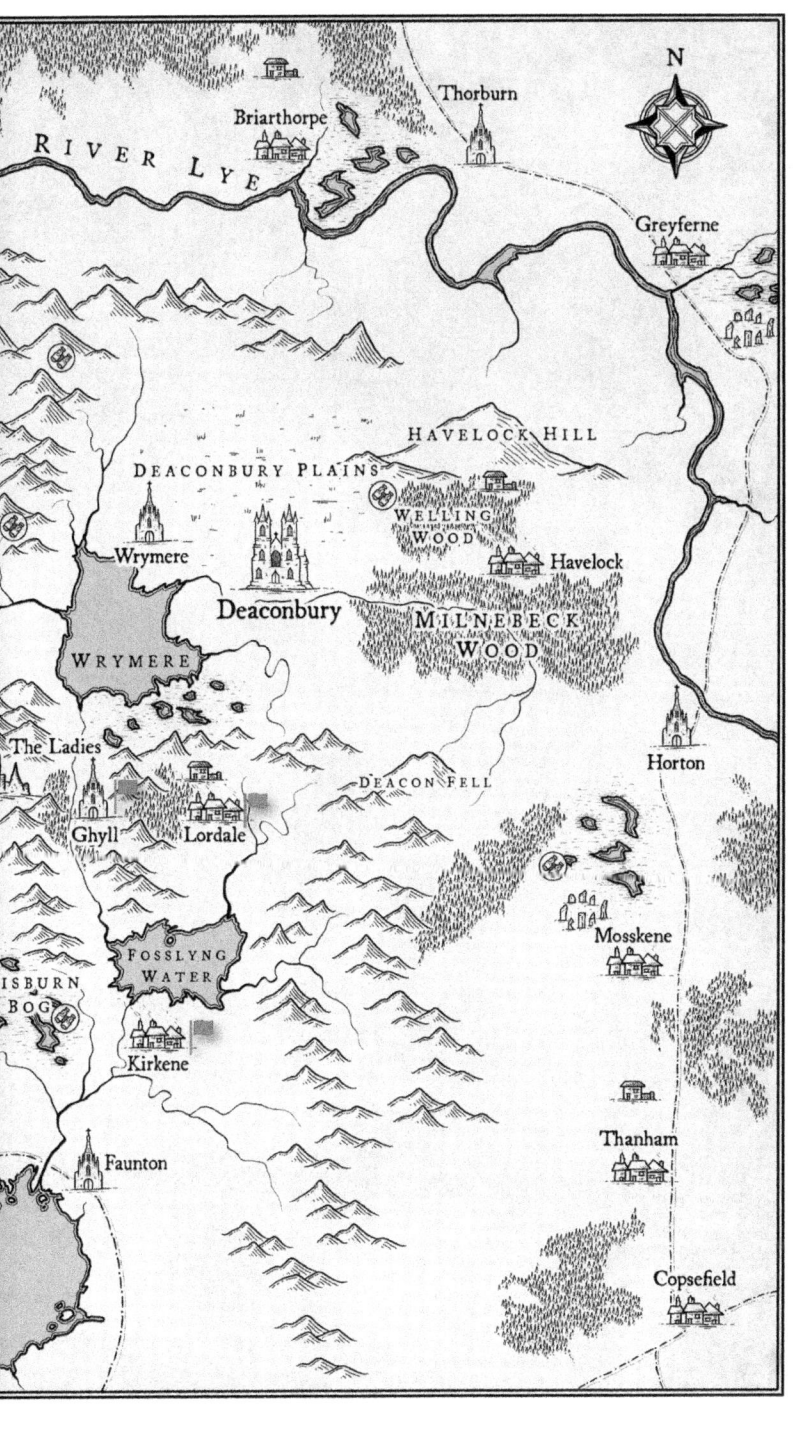

Contents

THE DREAM HOUSE

Autumn

WITHIN THE FOREST OF AUTUMN

Autumn, 2025

A giant of a man holds a card with my name on it. He wears a chauffeur's cap that doesn't quite fit his big round head, and he has somehow managed to squeeze himself into a suit. 'You must be Mr. Baylor,' I say as I approach the man. He lets out a grunt and walks off.

I follow the man out of the train station, where I am met by blue skies and a warmth that is uncharacteristic for mid-to-late autumn. Mr. Baylor guides me to an olive-green Jaguar and opens the back door.

'Nice! I didn't expect to be picked up in a classic car. Is this a Jaguar XJ from the '70s?' I ask. Mr. Baylor grunts again.

I am consumed by a ball of heat as I sit inside, placing my backpack in the adjacent footwell. The politeness of Mr. Baylor's door-opening gesture evaporates as he slams the door behind me. The black leather seats radiate heat, and the belt buckle burns my fingers as I click it in. Evidently, the car has been sitting in the sun for a while.

I manually wind down the window of this antiquated car to allow some of the trapped heat to escape. The Jaguar then lurches under Mr. Baylor's weight as he gets in. Mr. Baylor slams his own door shut, starts the engine, and then sets off with a jolt. A natural chauffeur this man is not.

As air blows in through the window, I stare out. Seagulls swirl and waves crash against rocks. I should have got off a stop earlier if I wanted a nice beach. Mr. Baylor turns off the coastal road and a smile grows on my face. The Deaconshire hills rise in the distance like a fantasy playground—my escape from reality. I shall spend the weekend hiking amongst those hills, but tonight I am staying with Mr. and Mrs. Baylor at Hawketh House.

I reach for my backpack, making sure I have the letters from Mrs. Baylor. She asked that I bring them as proof of correspondence. Exchanging handwritten letters is quite a novelty in this technological age. Her handwriting is almost illegible; I have to twist my head to every angle to decrypt her text. I love little touches of the past, but you also gain a new appreciation for modern simplicity.

Mrs. Baylor herself makes no apologies for not communicating online and she offers no telephone number; it was in my local newspaper that I found her advert and the address for her guest house. I have always liked old houses, and given its perfect location, I decided to send a letter. I was not expecting a cheap rate because she can afford to shun modern media, but the price she offered was more than reasonable.

In her messages, Mrs. Baylor expresses every desire to make my stay a *most remarkable* one. She said that the guest house had no menu but that Mr. Baylor would cook whatever I wished, nothing would be too much trouble. Appreciatively, I placed my order, and I have been looking forward to tonight's meal ever since.

Mrs. Baylor warned me about her husband, too. *He is a man of very few words*, she wrote, *but he will grunt once for yes and twice for no*. She also said that Mr. Baylor would be *all too pleased* to pick me up from the station. He doesn't appear to be pleased though—he seems more constipated than anything. I am grateful for the lift, however, as it allows me to see more of this historic county. I will hike all the way to Lyemouth, where I will get the train back home on Sunday.

A lake emerges on my right and stretches far into the distance. It mirrors the brilliant blue sky and the deep greens and browns of the hills that frame it. 'Is this Lake Linketh?' I ask Mr. Baylor.

He grunts once.

'Have you always lived beside the lake?'

He grunts twice.

'You must like living here.'

He doesn't make a sound.

The old, grainy photograph of the property in the newspaper showed Hawketh House at the far end of this lake, surrounded by a forest and hills—a perfect spot to hide from an ever-more intrusive world.

The browns and greens of the rolling hills soon become sprinkled with the magical dust of autumn as the burgeoning reds and ambers of an approaching woodland make a blazing entrance to the scene outside the car's windows. This county promises to provide a soothing retreat, which I have sorely needed for too long now.

I love the history and folklore of Deaconshire. Tomorrow, I shall see the castle where the Havelock Harpies were slain, and then I will spend Saturday night at a pub which supposedly lost many patrons to a mythical water horse. But I am most excited for tonight. Mrs. Baylor came across in her letters as wonderfully warm and pleasant, and she extolled the beauty of the creeper-clad house and its traditional charm inside.

We lose sight of the lake behind the wood, but its mosaic of yellows, ambers, browns and reds holds my wide-eyed stare. I gaze through the colourful leaves and dark tree branches trying to spy a house hidden somewhere inside, but the forest is so dense that I barely see further than a few metres. The car slows, and as my eyes scan, my heart leaps in tandem with bounding flurries of red that rustle the autumn leaves.

Two red squirrels are in a chase through the trees, running along the car's path, leaping from branch to branch. I've never seen a red squirrel before—and now here are two! Their furry tails are like an autumn paintbrush coating each of the leaves with their red dye as they brush past. Their majesty holds my eyes captive; this forest has already embraced me with wonder, and only now are we turning to enter it.

The entrance to the woodland is so hidden that branches and leaves scrape the car as we push through their barrier, but soon we are twisting and turning along a track that is a mix of mud and gravel. The breeze through the window turns cooler. I welcome it as I gaze up at a thick canopy glowing radiantly in its auburn hue as it holds back the sun. The leaves of the trees inside the forest are much greener—only their tips have been dipped in autumn. Occasional shafts of sunlight are the only rays to bring light to this gloomy forest floor. The red squirrels are out of sight now, but I spy rabbits hopping beside mushrooms before dashing through ferns when spooked by the car.

After a few minutes winding along this woodland track, I spy the lake once more. And then I see it—Hawketh House. The new chill in the air runs down my back, no longer welcome. The house stands alone beside the mere. Its walls are an unkempt patchwork of amber leaves and black slate. I study it closely as we approach. All its features exist in odd numbers: chimneys, gables, windows, storeys. And the ivy that crawls across its façade is unevenly spread. No birds fly to its perches and no creatures run to its shelter. Even the forest keeps its distance.

The car crunches the gravel as Mr. Baylor pulls in, and I gawp up at the ugly, irregular structure. I feel lightheaded—it's not unlike the blend of fear and dizziness you experience with vertigo. When Mr. Baylor parks, I wind up the window and step out slowly, ensuring I keep my balance.

The still lake pouts on one side and the house gurns on the other. The high hills look down upon me with a sympathetic stare. I follow Mr. Baylor to the entrance. A set of stone steps lead to a striking red front door surrounded by ivy. Atop the newel posts are two gargoyles, and they scowl at me as I climb. The sound of Mr. Baylor turning the key is loud and heavy, and the door groans open with the scrape of a sealed crypt. I enter Hawketh House.

THE HOUSE AT THE END
OF THE LAKE

The house is both opulent and crooked. A dark red rug runs the length of the hallway to a set of marble stairs that turns back on itself. Mahogany is the choice for the tables and sideboards. At the base of the stairs, a dark red curtain is roped open. It's unusual to see drapes across a room, but I suspect it's a means of preventing heat from escaping to the upper floors. Close to the curtain is a large landscape painting. It stands out because it's the only picture that sits straight. The walls are covered with oddly spaced landscapes and portraits that slant awkwardly and unevenly with each other, yet the painting by the curtain is the only one that appears to be treasured.

Feet descend the stairs. A flowing black dress drapes the bannister and soon divulges a slender physique. Where the stairs twist back, the figure turns and stops. The woman in black stares down at me coldly. 'Mr. Richmond, I presume,' she says.

'Yes, ma'am.'

'Follow me, please.'

She turns, and I follow her up the stairs. I begin to muse about how this quaint guest house must be a form of early retirement for the Baylors, but then something obscene grabs my attention. On the window ledge, where the marble stairs turn, are two porcelain ornaments: one is of a rabbit with red eyes and the other depicts a bowl of fish heads. Who on earth would wish to own such garish items?

Antiques, figurines, old photographs, and books fill the landing. A grandfather clock is hidden amongst shelves of more lurid statuettes. The doors to the rooms seem an inconvenience because they prevent more vintage ornaments from being displayed. Mrs. Baylor walks smoothly and slowly through the clutter, never once turning to check if I am following behind. Her hair is jet black and clings together in tight waves. Despite all the brash antiques, not a lick of colour touches her pasty white skin.

'You have a lovely house, Mrs. Baylor,' I say, hiding my distaste at the items on display. 'There is such a wealth of history within these walls.'

'Your room is on the top floor, Mr. Richmond.'

Mrs. Baylor leads the way through a narrow corridor and up a steep set of stairs. A terrible chill hits me at the top, and I stand in a dark converted attic. A blind is drawn to cover the only window but some light seeps up from below. There is a door to a room at either end and yet more jumble, although I spy a few diamonds in the rough. Mrs. Baylor opens the door to one of the rooms and steps inside. I follow her in, bowing my head where the door frame slants with the roof.

My room is long and the ceiling slopes on one side and at each end, one end being the bathroom. I have to be careful how I walk around so that I don't bump my head. The dormer windows act as pockets in the room where I can stand happily without arching my back. My view of the forest and hills is scenic, but I would have preferred to gaze over the length of the lake. I presume there must be other guests staying tonight because this room does not seem like any guest's first choice.

The room is hot too, yet Mrs. Baylor holds me in a gaze as frosty as the chill at the top of the stairs. She looks like a black-and-white film actress who has turned bitter and haggard with age but persists with the hairstyle of her youth. 'I think you shall find that you have everything that you desire here,' she says, 'thick robes, capacious wardrobes, heavy blankets and a bed that will cradle your sweet dreaming.'

'Thank you very much, Mrs. Baylor.'

'As for the house rules: evening meal will be served at seven in the dining room, first on the right at the bottom of the staircase; supper is at ten; lights out is midnight till six; there is no checkout time, but we can arrange a wake-up call. Now, do you have my letters of correspondence?' I fumble in my rucksack and hand them to her. 'Excellent, here is your key, and I shall leave you to make yourself comfortable.' I close the door behind her and test the cumbersome key in the lock, but there is no key for the front door. It is so quiet in the house that I hear the floorboards creak under Mrs. Baylor's light footsteps. Are there any other guests staying tonight?

My room is nearly as cluttered as the landing. There are three mahogany wardrobes, each a different style; several clocks telling the time of faraway places; dozens of dusty books; more unusual figurines; dreamcatchers that obscure the small windows; and curiously, a set of windchimes hanging by the bed. I understand that Mrs. Baylor wants her trinkets to be on display and not in boxes, but is there not a better place for wind-chimes?

Mrs. Baylor's persona in ink differs greatly to her persona in flesh. She seems like a lady you do not wish to upset, and I fear that moving her treasured possessions will do just that. It is so warm in here though that I need to open the windows. I must, therefore, remove the windchimes or they'll jangle in the breeze.

As I lift them off their hook, they burst into life with a grating, high-pitched clamour. I panic as I try to suppress the sudden sound, and I drop them. They crash to the floor like someone slumping on a piano. Mrs. Baylor will have heard that noise. I listen a moment for footsteps, thinking that she will tell me off, but all remains quiet.

I open the windows and welcome the breeze. The view is better now too, without the dreamcatchers obscuring it. The dreamcatchers are on all the windows, but that isn't the thing that strikes me as odd. The disks in the middle of them are not the typical meshed pattern like a spider's web, they are solid—I've never seen a solid dreamcatcher before. I try to search on my phone to see if it has any meaning, but I have no signal. Mrs. Baylor evidently believes in dreamcatchers and not Wi-Fi. There is no TV either, so I search the bookshelves for something interesting to read.

The books are a varied mix, both in genre and age. One of the newer books takes my interest: *The Truth of the Havelock Harpies* by Greg W F Finny. The highest point of my walk tomorrow will be Draymere Castle, the place where these supposed witches were hanged.

I take the book, and, thinking that it would be nice to read it outside, I leave my room. The house creaks as I retrace my steps down. I find the front door locked then look around for signs of life.

'Hello?' I call out. 'Hellooo?'

'Mr. Richmond.' I jolt as Mrs. Baylor appears behind me. 'Whatever is the matter?'

'I thought I'd go sit by the lake and read before dinner.'

'Very well, I shall ask Mr. Baylor to open up. Would you like a drink, perhaps a Gin Rickey to suit the sunny weather?'

'That would be lovely, thank you,' I say, and Mrs. Baylor ascends the marble stairs.

While I wait, I study the wonky paintings. There are many portraits of beautiful women wearing sparkly jewellery and pearl necklaces, and men in fedoras who frown like mobsters. Then I inspect the landscape which hangs at the base of the stairs, the one that sits straight. Many of the faces from the portraits appear in this landscape. The engraved plate on the frame reads *The Dream*.

The painting is of a gala and many happy faces smile at me as they cradle their partners. Some of the women wear glamourous headbands with a feather on one side, and there is a distinct 1920s feel to the fashion and style. Mrs. Baylor must have an interest in this era. Her hair is curled like the women in the canvas, and I believe a Gin Rickey is a drink that was popular back then.

I continue to stare at the painting, assessing the little historical details, when a hand on my shoulder startles me. 'Mrs. Baylor!' I gasp.

'Mr. Baylor is coming now. He will attend to your needs.'

When Mr. Baylor descends the stairs, he is half-dressed in a buttoned-up shirt but no tie. If they had given me a key, I wouldn't have had to inconvenience them. Mr. Baylor unlocks the door, pulls back several bolts and it screams open. There is no leaving this house quietly.

Mr. Baylor lets me out and shuts the door behind me again like I'm a dog taking a shit. Will I have to scratch to get back in?

I sit on the grass at the edge of the lake and marvel at its stillness and how its perimeter reflects the hills and autumn trees with such sharpness. I begin to read, but soon a shadow darkens the pages. Mr. Baylor is standing beside me, holding a small table in one hand and the cocktail in the other. He just stands there looking out towards the forest.

I wait a moment, expecting him to look down at me, but he does nothing. 'Thank you,' I say. 'You may put them down.' Mr. Baylor follows my order. I'd like to make the most of this free buffet and butler service, so I ask, 'Do you have any ice cream in the house at all?'

Mr. Baylor grunts once.

'Would it be okay if I had one?'

Mr. Baylor grunts once.

I doubt he is about to tell me a long list of options, so I say, 'Would you fetch me one, please? I like all flavours, so please surprise me with your selection.' Mr. Baylor nods, leaves, and returns with an ice cream moments later. Now who's the dog? What else can I get Mr. Baylor to fetch? He sees me smirk. 'Excellent choice,' I say, turning the smirk into a smile, 'you can't beat vanilla.'

Mr. Baylor just stands there again, staring above me with an unnaturally straight back like a Wimbledon ball boy. 'That will be all,' I say, deciding that ice cream and Gin is excessive enough. Mr. Baylor returns to the house. Those final words feel dirty in my mouth as though I have quickly become some unsympathetic member of the aristocracy, but I'm not going to enjoy the moment if he's standing over me.

I quickly discard the book and unwrap the ice cream. There is nothing nicer than Britain on one of these rare sun-kissed, autumnal days. While the lake rests peacefully, the woodland and surrounding hills blush with their seasonal colour. The only sound is the soft flutter of wings and the rustle of forest leaves. The sun warms and the ice cream cools. There is nothing better than right now.

After the ice cream, I lean back on my elbows, sip the cocktail and think.

I reflect on how lovely this moment is in contrast with the rest of my week. A mid-life crisis burns deep within me now, never letting me forget my unachieved dreams. History was always my passion; I went to university but ended up in insurance. So much for presenting *The World At War*; hell, I'd take *Bargain Hunt* now.

All I seem to do is push paperwork and get pushed around by the zealous new crop of graduates who know nothing of the work but are still able to trample their way up a ladder that I don't know how to climb. I think too of the frustration of attempting to date through vanity apps, and now I'm back to grumbling about how the world no longer values substance and character. I am an unsightly forty-one-year-old who has never had a promotion and now looks at the world not knowing what he wants anymore—except for this. Sitting here in the sun by a lake outside an old house and being waited on, this is good.

I read a chapter from the book about Alice Shelton, a kind-spirited woman who was hanged for being a witch because she stood in the way of greedy and entitled people who wanted her land, and I smile. I guess the world has always been like this.

A chill shivers through me and goosebumps run along my arm. Shadows of nearby trees stretch long and close to the house now. The temperature has dropped with the sun. I glance at the ancient woodland, and its mystical hue invites me. It will turn dark soon, but I'd like to catch another glimpse of those playful red squirrels.

It has been lovely sitting by the lake, but I drag myself to my feet. I stroll to the forest, and when the sun hides behind the canopy, the goosebumps on my arms flare in the cool, crisp air. I crunch fallen leaves on the ground, pressing them into the mud. I wander aimlessly, admiring the colours and searching for animals. I spy no fauna but an old tree stump acts as a hive for a burgeoning colony of white mushrooms.

I press a little further into the forest, but with the light fading, I vow not to venture too far. Each step is slow as I'm pushing through ferns or bushes as there is no path. It's not long before this forest of autumn provides another sprinkle of magic. Squeezing through a dense crop of ferns and foxgloves, I discover a verdant cluster of pixie toadstools. I've always associated these mushrooms—with their red and white-speckled caps—with fantasy. I inspect them closely, pondering what little mythical woodland creatures might call them home.

I consider turning back, but then I spy what looks like a path up ahead. I need to determine how to start my hike tomorrow, so it will be good to scout this path. Typically you will find footpaths around the lakes and meres of Deaconshire as hikers like to complete circular walks around them, but I've seen no sign of such a path around Lake Linketh.

To reach the start of the path, I duck below two low branches crossing two trees. I wander a few paces before pausing to observe a flurry of life. A hare hops away, a mouse scrambles in the undergrowth, small and brightly coloured birds dash left and right between trees, and a raven quorks overhead. I look upwards, searching the canopy. I then turn my body back towards the way I've come as I survey the treetops. Then, lowering my gaze, I lurch backwards, letting out a sharp cry.

Two scarecrows hang from two trees. In fact, the two branches that I ducked underneath are the arms of these scarecrows. My cry is partly out of surprise but also a result of their frightful aspect. Their gentle swaying in the light breeze affords the impression of hanged corpses. Straw stuffs two suits, and the more I look at them, I cannot help but wonder... Are those Mr. Baylor's suits?

There are no "Keep Out" or "Private Property" signs, but the scarecrows' position at the end of this footpath makes the point. And given how the flurry of wildlife is only on this side of the path, it implies that the animals understand this too.

A long shaft of light shines through the trees and I am suddenly fearful that I may be late for my evening meal. But now the fear isn't to miss a meal I have been highly anticipating—no, it is to ensure that I don't upset my hosts. Cautiously, I creep beneath the linked arms of the two dangling scarecrows, and I hurry back to Hawketh House. As I rush, I feel sympathetic eyes on my back from all the creatures who dare not follow me in crossing the boundary.

I remind myself that I still have time before the meal, but Mrs. Baylor said in her letters that she likes her guests to dress for dinner. I was not able to bring smart clothes in my backpack, but Mrs. Baylor offered to leave out clothes for me to wear. She said she had my size.

Beside the lake and amongst the patch of toadstools, serenity washed over me, but the sight of Hawketh House once more as I re-emerge from the wood claws it all away. It really is ugly, and as I stroll to the front door, I notice new details. All the upstairs curtains are closed, and why are there dreamcatchers on every single window? I know they are meant to ensure that you have pleasant dreams, but even if they do work, who is sleeping downstairs?

There are still no cars besides Mr. Baylor's either. If other guests are staying, I imagine they'd be back by now for the evening meal. I doubt Mrs. Baylor will serve someone who returns late.

The front door strains open before I can knock. Mr. Baylor is on the other side. Has he been waiting for me this whole time? And how did he know I was walking to the door? There is no peephole, and I didn't see him through the window. Perhaps he heard my footsteps.

In my room, I find a tuxedo in one of the "capacious" wardrobes. I do enjoy dressing up smart; it's fun to pretend that I am somebody of worth. I change and look in the mirror. I look good, or as good as I can look. The tuxedo may restrict my movement, but it forces me to hold my head high.

I am famished—I cannot wait for my meal. I take the key from the door and lock the room behind me. The house groans with my every step. I walk at a slower pace and peruse the antiques more closely. I suspect these are the collections of many different people, but only some had taste.

At the base of the stairs, I look again at *The Dream*. The way that I am dressed, I would fit right in. How wonderful and elegant that gala must have been. I look closer and spot something amiss. One of the guests is painted with a plastic wristwatch. They weren't around until the 1970s!

I follow Mrs. Baylor's directions to the dining room, but when I enter, I recognise it as something different. It is the ballroom from the painting. The curtains are closed, a fire burns low in the fireplace, and dozens of candles light the room. But there is something missing—something which I feared might be true. The room is empty, except for one table set for only one person. I am the only guest.

THE TELEGRAPH
MACHINE

I have been on my own most of my life such that it no longer bothers me. I will eat at restaurants by myself without hesitation, and with no other guests here, I am relieved of a self-conscious burden, and my eyes are freer to roam without the chance of awkwardly crossing paths with others. I feel lonelier when I'm on my own in a busy room than when there are no others, so what is it that's squeezing my stomach into a tight ball? It's not that I'm alone in this guest house but rather the isolation and lack of safety that comes in numbers.

But what do I have to fear? Do I offer anything that the Baylors might want? No, I don't offer anybody anything that they might want—that's why I'm always on my own. Might I just be letting my imagination get ahead of me when the only strangeness is that the house is older than most and the host's customs were moulded from a time that I never lived through? Absolutely.

The thought calms me, and I step into the room, taking a moment to survey this unique ballroom-turned-dining room. It is considerably more stylish than the jumble of gaudy trinkets upstairs. Everything is straight and neat and polished in here. Chandeliers and crystal-cut champagne flutes scatter the candlelight across vibrant blue walls. The furnishings are all mahogany, and blue and white vases sit on the mantel. A gramophone glints beside the door to the kitchen, and a telegraph machine, once used to send messages in Morse code, rests on the sideboard by my seat. Perhaps I am beginning to understand Mrs. Baylor. She is someone with a genuine fascination for the vintage, and she has the means to uphold the elegance of a time that most have moved away from due to cost and convenience.

Mrs. Baylor enters from the door that leads to the kitchen. 'Take your seat please, Mr. Richmond,' she instructs.

'Your eye for stylish antiques and traditional décor is exquisite, Mrs. Baylor,' I say. She does not respond. I sit at the table laid for one, and Mrs. Baylor fusses with putting the napkin on my lap. 'I saw that this room has been immortalised in the painting at the bottom of the stairs,' I say to dispel the awkward silence hanging between us. 'I'm curious as to when it was painted and by whom?'

'I painted it, Mr. Richmond. Your starter will be ready shortly.'

'Oh wow! You are extremely talented.' I don't have the heart to mention her anachronistic error, though.

Mrs. Baylor ignores my praise and retrieves a wine bottle from a display cabinet. 'For something to drink,' she says, 'may I make a recommendation—a 1976 Bonnes Mares vintage?'

Such a fine wine would be lost on me, but I think it would offend Mrs. Baylor if I decline. 'You truly are a wonderful hostess, Mrs. Baylor,' I say as I perform the awkward ritual of approving the drop which she pours for me.

'Where is home to you, Mr. Richmond?' Mrs. Baylor asks as she pours me half a glass.

'I've travelled from Manchester. Have you always lived here?'

'You live alone, do you not? No wife or children?'

'No.'

'No husband either? This is a modern world supposedly.'

I chuckle, 'No, no husband.'

'Then who are you close to?'

'I do have friends and family, Mrs. Baylor,' I reply, a little affronted.

'Did you tell any of them about this house?'

'I told them I was coming to Deaconshire for the weekend, but that was all,' I reply, curious as to why she asked.

'Good.'

'Why's that good?' I challenge her.

'We don't like to advertise ourselves too much as I'm sure you've gathered.'

'I don't think my friends and family would understand the appeal of your house. The idea of leaving technology behind would seem silly to them, I expect.'

'Yes, quite. We do not allow just anyone to stay. A guest must be a good fit for this house.'

'Do you get many guests?'

'Not many. I do not need the money, in truth, Mr. Richmond, but I like to share this house with those who would appreciate it—those who look twice at a non-descript newspaper advertisement about a historic house and then follow this up with a letter. But it cannot just be any letter; the type of person suited to this house would handwrite the letter with a fountain pen. This house is a special place, Mr. Richmond, and I intend to keep it that way.'

'Absolutely,' I say. It is a strangely specific requirement, though. 'When did you last have a visitor?'

'A most gracious woman stayed three nights ago, but before that, we hadn't had a guest for nine months.'

'Nine months?' Why on earth am I stuck in the attic room if there's only been one other guest in nine months?

'That's right. That guest, unfortunately, was not right for this house. But never mind. Are you ready for your appetiser?'

'Yes please,' I say, and Mrs. Baylor leaves the room.

I didn't realise that I was so privileged to stay here. As I swill the wine and savour the aroma, as I feel I ought, I regard the room in a new way. Hawketh House is more exclusive than a royal palace. Staying here should feel like a privilege, but her odd line of enquiry unnerves me once more. And why did she ignore my questions?

I cannot help thinking that Mrs. Baylor has misjudged me. I do like old places and traditions, like writing with a fountain pen, but I am not a person of class or elegance. I couldn't say anything insightful about the paintings on the wall or the subtle notes in the wine. And while I believe there are elements of the Art Deco style throughout the downstairs, I'm not confident enough to assert it.

I can imagine many people see this house from the other end of the lake and wonder what lies inside. I reach for my phone in my pocket to take a picture, but, hearing footsteps, I quickly put it back.

Mrs. Baylor arrives with a plate of smoked salmon roulade. 'Mrs. Baylor, this looks fantastic,' I say. 'Thank you very much.'

Mrs. Baylor looks up, but she glances over my shoulder towards the telegraph machine, and says, 'I expect your judgement very soon,' and then she leaves. Another odd thing to say. The food will be lovely, I have no doubt. But I suppose if your only conversation in nine months is with a man who can only grunt then I suspect you would struggle to talk conventionally.

I take out my phone and snap a picture of my food. If I were more sophisticated, I wouldn't dream of doing such a thing. I take a few snapshots around the room too to capture all the quirky details, like the gramophone and the telegraph, and then I tuck in.

The salmon melts in my mouth. It is delicious, and before I know it, it is gone.

'That was delightful, Mrs. Baylor,' I say as she collects the plate.

'Are you ready for your main course, Mr. Richmond?'

'Yes, ma'am.'

Mrs. Baylor brings in a giant plate of haggis, neeps and tatties. My taste buds remember the first time I ate it in Fort William. It is sensational, and I start wolfing it down.

Whilst I am eating, Mrs. Baylor returns. She walks up to me calmly. I can see she is about to ask me a question, but I have my mouth full.

She looks past me as before and asks, 'What's the judgement?'

BEEP!

The noise is from the telegraph machine.

'Very well,' Mrs. Baylor says. She exits to the hallway, and I hear her trample up the stairs.

What just happened? Was she asking me about the food? I haven't said a word. Why did the telegraph machine beep? I turn to look at it; it rests still. I follow the wires. It is connected, so it can beep, and it definitely did beep, just once though.

I swallow my mouthful and check my phone. I'm not sure what I'm looking for, but I flick through the pictures until I get to the photo with the telegraph. Part of the photo is a blur like a heat haze on a desert horizon. I quickly take another—again a blur. I move the lens and the picture is clear, but then, when I take another image of the telegraph machine, my phone shuts down indicating zero battery. It had plenty of charge when I came downstairs.

Windchimes! The tinkle of metal ivories fills the house. Mrs. Baylor is in my room! Her footsteps creak high above. I knew she would not like me taking them down, but how dare she enter my room without asking.

I stare at my half-eaten meal; my appetite has vanished. Mrs. Baylor is in my room, this house is making strange noises, and the only other person cannot or does not speak. I was led to believe this was a guest house, but this is just some weirdo's home. How can I expect to sleep if I think Mrs. Baylor might walk in on me?

Her footsteps descend, and I follow her sound through the house. Do I dare confront her? No, it will not be wise to anger her. She enters.

'Mr. Richmond,' she starts, 'you must know one thing: everything in this house has its place for a reason. I trust that you will see that nothing is moved. It is *very* important,' she adds with a stare, as if I should grasp some hidden meaning from it. I grasp nothing. She breaks her gaze and walks toward the kitchen door. 'Please continue your meal,' she says, calmly. 'I would hate for you not to enjoy it.' She returns to the kitchen.

For fear of further confrontation with Mrs. Baylor, I eat. She is up to something, knows things, and appears in utter control of whatever is going on. Her actions, while odd, seem to have purpose and precision. Why did she insist that Mr. Baylor pick me up when I could have driven here? Why was she asking if anyone knew where I was? If I had signal and battery, I would message someone. Mrs. Baylor even insisted that I bring her letters. The outside world has no idea that I am here, and she knows that now. Silently I make a vow: do nothing to anger Mrs. Baylor.

SWEET DREAMING

A fter I finish my main course, Mrs. Baylor brings me dessert. A sticky toffee pudding glistens gluttonously—my favourite! A disturbing thought enters my mind... Is Mrs. Baylor treating me like a death-row prisoner? Why else would she let me choose whatever meal I wanted?

When Mrs. Baylor returns to the kitchen, I survey the room. It perfectly mirrors the painting, with the exception that there's no moonlight and the curtains are closed. Might there be some clue as to what the nature of this house is hidden in some of the cupboards or drawers?

I creep to a cupboard and open it slowly and quietly. All I see is crockery. Next, I open a drawer, but I hear footsteps and rush back to my chair. I return before Mrs. Baylor notices.

'Mr. Richmond, are you not hungry?'

'No, no—I am hungry,' I say, flustered.

'But you haven't touched your dessert, Mr. Richmond. Is it not what you wanted?'

'No, no—it's perfect. I was letting my dinner settle for a moment.'

'Very well, Mr. Richmond,' she says and leaves.

My nerves are shot, but I do savour my pudding as if it's the last thing I will ever eat.

I try to hide my worry by not going back to my room immediately after finishing my pudding. Instead, I sip my wine and compliment Mrs. Baylor a great many times. She seems disinterested in me now. I say a final, 'Thank you,' and head upstairs.

On the first floor, I sense the eyes of the vintage dolls and figures in photographs are upon me. I hurry through, trying not to meet their gaze, then scuttle up the attic stairs. But, at the top, an icy breath blows right through me. I shiver and nearly fall. Once I reach the door to my room, the frosty chill is gone.

I scramble inside, lock the door then lean against it and exhale with a heavy sigh. My backpack is by my feet, and I hastily search the pockets. I find my penknife, pull out the longest blade and place it beneath the pillow on the bed. The windchimes are back up and the windows are shut, but the room is not so hot now. I sit on the soft bed and anxiety consumes me. I can't wait to leave this freakish place.

My concern only deepens. I try to snap out of it by standing up and changing out of my tuxedo into one of the robes provided. Outside, the stars are shining above swathes of blackness formed by the hillside. A brightness illuminates the hilltop horizon, signalling that the moon will rise soon. The thought of walking along that ridgeline tomorrow excites me, but I have to get through a night in this house first. I pull the curtains closed, pace up and down along the narrow corridor of headspace then sit back on the bed.

I listen to the sounds below. Hawketh House intends to let everyone know where everyone is. Mrs. Baylor is on the first floor, at the top of the stairs. I hear a key clank in a lock; a door creaks open and the floorboards groan as she enters one of the rooms. I track her movements. She crosses the room... comes back out... locks the door... unlocks another room... enters... comes out... turns the key again... and so on into every room on the first floor. What is she doing? Why would she need to enter all the unoccupied bedrooms? No one is coming to stay, not if I'm only the second visitor in nine months.

The sound of Mr. Baylor washing and clinking the dishes brings some sense of normality. My nerves start to settle. In fact, I smile at how agitated I've become. Such a peculiar place messes with your mind. Mrs. Baylor has no reason to want to attack me or enter my room tonight; she just likes things the way they are. Plus, I know an easy way to keep her out. I will leave the key in the lock.

I recharge my phone, but text messages still won't send. I study the hazy blur in the photos. It must be the mirror beside the telegraph machine reflecting candlelight onto the lens. What else did I think it was? A ghost? I really let my imagination get the better of me.

———◦———

I'd almost forgot about supper, but when I go back down, Mrs. Baylor offers me a choice of cold meats and a variety of cheeses and pâtés together with crackers. Eating again is a welcome reminder that dinner was not my last meal. Mrs. Baylor also offers me a nightcap—a nice peaty scotch—and I compliment her on her taste once more.

'Mr. Richmond, what time would you like breakfast in the morning?' she asks.

'7 a.m., please. I wish to get an early start.'

'And would you like Mr. Baylor to knock on your door as a wakeup call?'

'Yes please, 6 a.m.?'

'Very well. That is arranged. Mr. Richmond, after you have supped, please leave your plates there and Mr. Baylor will clear them away. And remember, lights out is midnight.'

'Yes, Mrs. Baylor. I won't be any trouble.'

'Very good. I shall retire for the evening now. Sweet dreaming, Mr. Richmond.' To my surprise, a kind smile curls on her face as she walks out.

This time when I go back to my room, I take my time. Mrs. Baylor, believing in a time before electric light, has lit many candles. I like it. The soft glow makes everything that bit more peaceful and placid. And yes, there are strange ornaments and dolls and paintings and monochrome photographs that all stare, but they don't seem sinister now. Part of the thrill of visiting an old house is indeed that—the thrill. Hawketh House has allowed my imagination to run wild, for which I now feel grateful. My body had almost forgotten what it was like to feel adrenaline.

I still sense the deathly cold patch in the attic, though. I felt it on my way down for supper too. But I've heard of things like this. Old houses have hot and cold spots. It's just how they are.

I pace back and forth. The temperature change is re-markable. I put my hand to the floorboards, suspecting a cool draught from below, but I can't feel one. Perhaps it's coming down from the roof. Whatever it is, it is not harming me. I go into my room, making sure to keep the key in the locked door—just in case.

———◇———

Seven to midnight and my lights are out. I crawl into a very comfy bed. Perhaps it is the wine and whisky and gin, but my earlier concerns seem laughable. I think back to how Mrs. Baylor said, 'A bed that will cradle your sweet dreaming.' I like that thought. This is the perfect bed in which to let the hours slide by. Sleep comes quickly.

———◇———

I jolt up in my bed. The windchimes are jangling! I draw my penknife and flick on the bedside lamp. Its light dispels all remnants of sleep. The room is empty, yet the windchimes are swaying. On the ceiling, shadows dance to their tune. I rush out of bed and go to the door. It remains shut with the key in the lock. I put my hand beside it, then all around the cracks in the door, then by the windows. I check everywhere—no draught. Perhaps it was a random gust of wind. I look at the beam where the windchimes hang and the ceiling above for something else that might have disturbed them, but there's nothing. I unlock the door and open it.

I gaze out at the attic landing. A dreamcatcher fixed to the door of the guest room opposite stares back at me.

'Hello?' I whisper.

Silence. The windchimes are still now. Did they really move? Nothing stirs out in the landing, so I shut the door and lock it again. I look once more at the windchimes. Could a creature have disturbed them? The room is as still as it was when I went to sleep.

I check the time: 2.08 a.m. I sit on the edge of the bed. I struggle to think. My head is foggy, a rhythm of words loops round and round: *Ten cents a dance...*

Where's that come from? A song on the radio? But I haven't listened to the radio today. As many times as I repeat those words, I can't make out where it's come from. I think I'm just tired. The windchimes look at me, innocent and still. I'm sure they jingled, but how? I'm not thinking straight; they can't have done. My mind is playing tricks on me because this is a spooky house. I try to sit quietly so I can think, but the ticking clocks won't allow me my sanity.

I get up, go to the bathroom and have a drink. The cold water slides down my throat and wakes more of my senses. I am fully awake now and rational thought returns. The words no longer repeat in my head, and I am quite sure that there is nothing here to hurt me.

I check the room once more and get back into bed. I turn the light off and replace the penknife under the pillow.

I lie awake and all remains quiet, besides the ticking clocks which are annoyingly out of sync with each other. Nonetheless, sleep creeps up on me again, and soon, it carries me away.

THE PICTURE ON THE WALL

Red eyes stare. The porcelain rabbit beside the fish-heads ornament gazes at me. Music draws me down the stairs: a jolly piano, a smooth saxophone, a subtle cello and the song of a passionate woman. Old-time jazz is another peculiar interest of mine. It stirs a sense of melancholy in me. I think for people who are offered so little by the modern world, we harbour a bizarre nostalgia for times we never lived through. Excitement overrides such longing now though as I'm fascinated to find out what's going on down there.

Descending the stairs feels like a memory. It is a strange, senseless experience. Each step is utterly silent too; the house is not groaning now. The curtains at the base of the stairs are closed, but there is chatter on the other side. Their voices bounce happily and heartily. It is the friendly clamour of an exclusive party. It may be inviting, but will they let me join? At the base of the stairs, I reach out to open the curtains, but my hand goes through. Before I know what's happened, I emerge on the other side.

The hallway is full of candlelight and partygoers. Many of the guests cluster and talk while a few couples sway to the music. Several look my way, and one of the women breaks off and walks towards me. Her hair is blonde, but it shines and curls like leaves of gold. A black headband runs across her forehead and fastens at the side with a silver brooch and a few black feathers. She wears a sleek black dress that stops at her knees. I believe she is what is known as a "flapper", an icon of the Roaring Twenties. A seductive smile grows as she approaches.

'Welcome, Mr. Richmond. I believe you are familiar with this painting,' she says, gesturing to the picture titled *The Dream*. 'Allow me to invite you in.'

My head is foggy and all I can think to say is, 'Thank you. It's quite a party you're having.'

'You are dressed most handsomely, I must say.'

I look down and realise that I am wearing the tuxedo I wore to dinner. I pull a face in confusion. It's as though I'm trying to clear the fog in my head, but all I'm able to do is make it swirl around me. I look back to the painting, wondering why I'm still dressed like the men on the canvas, and then I pause. Dumbstruck, I stare and lean in. I then point to the woman at the centre of *The Dream*, and say, 'Is this you?'

'It is, my dear. Now, won't you join me for a dance?' She offers her hand then leads me through to the room where I had dinner and supper.

My table is gone, and the dining room has been turned back into a ballroom. The curtains are now open and moonlight streams through the windows. Dreamcatchers hang on these windows too, and the lunar rays add a cool and ethereal tone to the warmth offered by the vast array of candles. It is a large but crowded space, and I pause a moment to take in what I am seeing.

This is the scene in the painting, except everyone is dancing rather than facing me, or rather, the artist. In my tuxedo, I can join in and pretend as though I am there in the picture. My hostess turns and smiles. I look at her in astonishment, then glance at the singing gramophone.

'Do you like the music, Mr. Richmond?' she asks.

'I love it!' I beam, and she smiles.

'Tonight, we dance to Ruth Etting. Would you care to join me?'

'Dance?' I say. 'I'm not sure how.'

'I think you are better than you realise. Here,' she puts my hands on her hips and cradles her arms around me. We sway. I fall into the rhythm. 'You've done this before,' she says with a grin. I smile back, surprised at how natural this all seems.

The song is slow but exhilarating. We sway towards the fireplace, and though it is just ashen embers, it is hot. Feeling the heat convinces me that this is truly happening. I caress my hostess' contours and hold her close.

'I know this song!' I say with delight.

The young woman before me beams. She's damn gorgeous! 'As I've just said,' she says, 'you've done this before.'

'I have?'

'Yes. Don't you remember me?'

'How could I not remember you?' I say. But I don't remember her.

'You are very sweet.'

'I think you might be the girl of my dreams—'

'More than you know,' she cuts in, biting her lip.

'—but, this is embarrassing, I don't recall your name.'

'Well, my dear, my name is Miss Agatha Downing. Do you like it here?'

'Absolutely!'

'What if I told you that you never had to leave?'

The song changes, and trumpets blare into life. The mood of the room jolts. It becomes a carnival. 'This is a particular favourite of ours,' Agatha says. 'Are you ready?'

'Ready?' I ask.

Agatha grins, and she leads me in a much livelier dance. I know this song too. It's called "Button Up Your Overcoat". My feet chase hers, and our bodies dash. I stumble, and Agatha laughs, but soon I am racing to the rhythm—I am swinging!

I toss Agatha every which way and the two of us are in perfect sync. My body spins as fast as my head. And it's not just because of the gorgeous blonde with whom I dance. The whirling scene around me bewilders. It is a mesmerising medley of colours: oranges and pinks and yellows and blues and reds. Mostly it is from the vibrant dresses and hats of the youthful women, but it is enhanced by the colourful stripes in the men's suits. It is also a display of sophistication: trilbies and headbands; bow ties and pearls; hair gel and curls. An array of rings and jewellery creates quite a sparkle too.

Then an instrumental comes on and there is a hell of a hullabaloo. Most of the men break from their partners and put great energy into their "air" trumpeting. Their partners, meanwhile, take the opportunity to dance and prance and giggle with their fellow girls. The laughter of youthful women never fails to tantalise men. I, myself, dance through it all—hardly able to take my eyes off them, hardly able to take my eyes off my golden girl. The trumpet sings and my heart tingles.

When the solo breaks, the regular dancing resumes. Tangos and foxtrots have never moved me, but here they are in full flow. I fall in step and rejoice as if I have discovered a new religion. Many of the women smile at us, while several men tip their hats and look on jealously. After all, I am dancing with the most beautiful woman in the room. Exhilaration fills me. All the couples swirl and twirl; I have never felt so alive. Joy and elation are emotions that I have rarely experienced, yet here they are, loud and proud. I have enjoyed jazz occasionally over the years, but on those nights, I danced alone. With all these people, tonight might just be the best night of my life!

The pace of the room eases as another slow song comes on. I gaze longingly at Agatha and do not hesitate to hold her close once more.

'I see why you enjoy that song,' I say.

'I love the trumpets,' Agatha says.

'Me too!' I say with great excitement. 'I've never been to a place like this before.'

'We'd love to have you here,' Agatha says.

'Do you know artists like Al Bowlly and Gene Austin?' I ask.

'We dance to them all the time.'

'Did you say I never have to leave?' I joke.

'That's right.'

'Then I must be dreaming!' I say with a laugh.

'You said, quite flatteringly, that I am the girl of your dreams. Well, I am pleased to tell you that this dream never has to end.'

Agatha smiles. I think she's teasing me. I narrow my eyes and survey the ballroom in an attempt to figure out what's going on. A plastic wristwatch on one of the men dancing catches my eye. I recognise him from the painting too. I'd judged Mrs. Baylor to have made an anachronistic error by painting such a watch—but what if she didn't make a mistake? The fog in my head swirls faster and faster. What is it that Mrs. Baylor painted? And why do I find myself in it?

'You look worried, my dear,' Agatha says.

'Is this real?'

'Come,' Agatha breaks off our dance and leads me towards the table with the telegraph machine and the mirror. 'What do you see?' she points to the mirror in front of us.

'Nothing...' I say with a tremble in my voice. The mirror reflects an empty room!

'So you think this isn't real?'

'How can it be? Am I actually dreaming?'

'Watch.' She hits the telegraph.

BEEP!

My mouth drops open. I stare at Agatha.

'Did you enjoy your meal?' she asks.

'My meal?'

'Do you recall Mrs. Baylor asking for a judgement?'

'Yes. Mrs. Baylor was talking to *you*? I thought she was asking me if the food was good.'

'Of course, you did, but she was asking me if I wanted to admit you to The Dream. I tapped once for yes.'

I hit the telegraph but there's no sound. 'Harder,' Agatha instructs. I hit it with force.

BEEP!

I recoil in shock. I go to pick up the machine. I can't. I try to grab a letter opener sitting on the table. I can't. In fact, my hand goes through the table.

'This isn't real. I am dreaming.' I pinch myself and feel numb.

'This is both real and a dream.'

'How?'

'You dream every night, do you not?' Agatha asks. I nod, dumbly. 'Why is that not real?'

'Because...' I struggle to find the words. How do I explain that something which every single person experiences is not real?

'Was the beep of the telegraph at dinner not real?' Agatha beams and I remain tongue-tied. 'What would you say, Mr. Richmond, if I said I could offer you immortality?'

'I would ask what you were smoking?'

Agatha giggles. She looks away and then back up at me with that sultry grin. I'm not sure I have any power to resist this temptress. 'It is possible,' she says. 'Especially in *this* house.'

'How?'

'What do you think a dream is?'

'I don't know.'

'Do you believe in spirits, Mr. Richmond?'

'Like whisky and gin?'

'No,' she tilts her head as if I am teasing her. 'Some people call them ghosts.'

'I never have.'

'When you sleep, your spirit is free to roam. What you see and experience as a spirit is what you dream.' Agatha raises an eyebrow. 'A dream can be real, and a spirit never has to die—don't you see? The Dream is eternal!'

'How can it be real?'

'Mr. Richmond, did you hear something tonight—something real?' Agatha smirks like a magician ready to reveal a trick.

'Like...?'

'Windchimes... In your bedroom...'
'Yes! They woke me up. What made them move?'
'Mr. Richmond, you made them move.'

THE SPIRIT OF NEW ORLEANS

A gatha walks across the ballroom and beckons me to follow, but I stand rooted to the spot. I'm still reeling from the notion that I moved the windchimes that woke me up. Those chimes gave me quite the fright. Did I spook myself? My mind spins as fast as the dancing couples.

I chase Agatha and ask, 'Are you sure that I rang the windchimes?'

'Yes, Mr. Richmond,' Agatha replies without breaking her stride.

'Why would I ring them?'

'Because you have a choice.'

'A choice?'

'You have a choice as to whether you wish to remain in The Dream. The windchimes are there to wake you up should you wish to leave.'

'What do you mean, "leave"? I will wake up soon, anyway.'

'Only if you choose to, Mr. Richmond.'

'That doesn't make any sense,' I say.

Agatha approaches a man loitering beside the gramophone. He is the only black man in the room, and his dreadlocks and snazzy waistcoat impress. 'Ah, Mr. Darcantel,' she says, 'let me introduce you once more to Mr. Richmond.'

'Is good to meet you again.' He speaks with a strong accent. 'Call me, Christophe, you hear me.'

'I've met you before?'

'Yeah son, but I know you don't remember.'

'Why wouldn't I remember?'

''Cause nobody don't ever remember their dreams, son. But that's a good thing, 'cause it means this secret don't ever leave these walls.'

'Has no one ever remembered their dream of this place?'

'Oh, yeah someone did once.' Christophe points to a man with blond hair in a tuxedo like mine. 'That's Geoffrey over there. We call him "the man who woke up". He thanks the Lord every day, you hear me, every day. Mr. Baylor said something for him to remember.'

'Mr. Baylor spoke?' I ask.

'I ain't lying. They were the last words he ever said,' Christophe says with a chuckle.

Agatha interrupts, saying, 'Mr. Darcantel has been here since 2004, is that correct?' I catch Agatha shoot Christophe a sharp glance.

'Yes ma'am, that's correct. I ain't going like never leave this place, you know. I don't never regret it.'

'You don't regret what?'

'Not waking up, you hear me. I was over in this country selling caws, son, and I was good at it.'

'Caws?'

'Cars,' Agatha states.

'Ah.'

Christophe continues, 'I liked this country, son, and most people liked me, once they got used to me like. I thought I had my whole life ahead of me, son. Then I came here, and I realised something.'

'What was that?'

'That I could have more than my whole life ahead of me. And what was my life? Yo, I was jacking people's money every day, with a smile too, you know.' Christophe chuckles. 'And for what? A shiny caw? A big house? Nah, that shit don't soothe the soul, you know. I was looking for some swanky ass place for a vacation, and I found this. I play the jazz, you know, and I put that in my letter. And in New Orleans, we used to hidden places, but never did I think I'd find such a place here. And what a place this is. This place is full of some interesting people, son. Let me introduce you.' Christophe taps a smart, clean-shaven man behind him on the shoulder, and says, 'Yo, this here is Mr. Richmond. Say hi.'

The man looks a little startled, but says, 'Good to meet you.'

'Yo, this man was a banker. Tell him what your bonus were,' Christophe says.

'My annual bonus was a little shy of a million pounds,' the man says.

'Why did you stay here?' I ask.

'This place—this dream—money cannot buy you something like this,' he says.

Christophe then taps the person next to him on the shoulder and says to me, 'Do you recognise this man?'

'No,' I reply.

'Exactly! This man was set to be a big star in one of those old films, but he came here and decided to stay. It ain't just old people who stay here, son.' Old people? There are no old people here.

'Good to meet you,' the man says. He's a handsome chap, wearing a dazzling pinstripe suit and a boatman hat.

'And why did you stay?' I ask the man.

'Oh, I just loved the place, but damn if I didn't join at the perfect moment. The world rather took a turn for the worse as I joined before the Second World War, and I don't much like what has re-emerged either. But what I love remains firm and unchanging in The Dream.'

'Thank you, fellas,' Christophe says. Then he turns to me, and adds, 'I don't want you thinking that I'm just picking stooges. Pick someone for yourself and I'll introduce you.'

The decision does not take long. There is a young man in a plain tuxedo, but he wears a Fez. That is enough to stir my intrigue, so I point him out.

'Oh. That there is Lyle Peters,' Christophe says. 'He's a musician.'

We walk over.

'What instrument did you play?' I ask Lyle after Christophe gives us a brief introduction.

'Ah. I played many, young man,' Lyle says with an exceedingly posh accent. 'The trombone, cello, bugle, but the trumpet was what I was known for. A friend of Miss Downing I was.'

'Mr. Peters' charm has never faded,' Agatha adds.

'So, why did you stay?' I ask.

'Don't be silly, I could never refuse. Agatha waited until old age crept devilishly close before summoning me here. I was to kick the bucket sooner or later. So

I decided later, an eternity later.' Lyle gives a hearty chuckle. 'Don't be daft now, young man, come join us.'

'I'm certainly thinking about it,' I say politely. Myself, Agatha and Christophe leave Lyle to dance. Such praise is hard to refute. 'How did this all come about?' I ask them.

'It was your father who discovered it in my hometown, weren't it?' Christophe says to Agatha.

'Discovered what?' I ask.

'There is a house in New Orleans,' Christophe says with a smirk.

'Yes,' Agatha cuts in. 'My father's love for jazz took him there. It is a house much like this, and he was a guest. Though, he decided to wake up because he didn't want to leave me with the nanny. Despite forgetting his dream, he was captivated by the house there.

'Christophe, did you not have any hesitation about staying here yourself?' I ask.

'Yeah, son, I rang them chimes.' Christophe laughs. 'Son! Everybody rings them chimes once. I ain't known anybody who ain't ring them chimes. And it's funny, 'cause y'all don't remember nothing. But listen to me, son.' His face turns serious. 'Since that day, I've had the best time dancing and singing and swaying. I have no anger, you hear me, only joy. Every night, son, I swing and my soul sings. You'll feel welcome here, allow me to show you.' Christophe turns to the gramophone, then he hits the needle up. The music stops.

'Ladies and gentlemen!' he announces to the guests, 'Let me introduce to you, for the second time... Mr. Richmond! I said y'all'll make him feel welcome.'

Shouts come back at me from the crowd:

'Stay, Mr. Richmond.'

'Come dance with me, Mr. Richmond.'

'You can live forever, Mr. Richmond.'

I sheepishly smile back at the beaming faces.

'Now then,' Christophe continues, 'it's time for Mr. Richmond's second first dance.' Christophe hits the gramophone's arm hard on the side. It moves just a touch towards the edge of the record, much less than I thought it would have from his powerful strike. Christophe sees my puzzled expression. 'A spirit's touch is like a waft of a feather,' he says. 'Try it, son. Hit the needle down, real hard like.'

I whack the needle; it falls softly onto the spinning disc record. A new song bursts into life. Agatha offers her hand, inviting me to dance once more. The crowd parts as she leads me to the centre of the ballroom—we have an audience. It's a slow song, and I know the lyrics: *Ten cents a dance...*

Agatha and I sway. She rests her head on my chest, and I hold her close again. The crowd cheers. Once more I feel exhilaration. Not only does it seem like the first dance at a wedding, but I also think I may have just made a very big commitment. I don't believe in heaven, but if I did, it might not look too far from this. Agatha hypnotises me, Christophe is full of charm, the others that I've met are unanimous in their joy, and everyone here is young and beautiful and happy.

Agatha's bright green eyes gaze up at mine. Such a woman of beauty and vintage grace would not exist in the real world, but here we can dance forevermore. I feel so privileged that she invited me. I need not worry anymore about mortal hassles or stress about promotions or feeling glum about having turned forty with my life in a rut. Mrs. Baylor was right to ask about whether I had a family because, having no children or spouse, I am free to accept such an opportunity. The next song comes on and everyone else joins in.

I revel in the rhythm for several more songs, but questions grow increasingly in my mind, so I pull Agatha aside.

'Do you always play jazz music?' I ask.

'Mrs. Baylor chooses the record each night,' Agatha explains, 'but it is usually popular music from the '20s, '30s and '40s.'

'And do you use the telegraph to talk to Mrs. Baylor?'

'Only when there are guests. Mr. and Mrs. Baylor will usually join us for our nightly dance, but not when guests are staying. She quite rightly worries that a guest who decides to wake will remember them from The Dream and then know The Dream to be real. Mr. Richmond, let me introduce you to one last person.'

In this whirlwind of new faces, Agatha introduces another suave young man in a pinstripe suit. She hugs him and says, 'Oh, papa. I want you to meet our new guest, Mr. Richmond.'

'Ah, Mr. Richmond,' he says, 'It's great to meet you. I see my daughter has already taught you how to dance.'

'I never thought it possible,' I say, 'but your daughter is a wonderful teacher. I must say, though, are you not a little young to be her father?'

'We all remain young in The Dream, Mr. Richmond.'

'How come?'

'The spirit takes the form of how we like to imagine ourselves—our dream selves, so to speak.'

'It's so enchanting. You have created a wonderful place here, Mr. Downing.'

'Oh, this is my dear daughter's creation. I just stumbled upon something when I returned from New Orleans. I see you've met Christophe.' I nod. 'He discovered this house, and we were keen to welcome him as he brings some of the spirit of the place. But I also brought these bizarre dreamcatchers back from New Orleans. The house out there had them on all the windows and doors. I loved the style, and I was fascinated by their Native American origins and their beliefs. I procured enough to fill Hawketh House. And even though I didn't subscribe to their beliefs, I was persuaded to buy "real" ones, created by Native shamans—as they supposedly held the secret to making them "work". Later I modified them to the style of those in that house. When I put them up here, I made the mistake of putting one on my bedroom door without knowing what they did.

'What do they do?'

'Your typical dreamcatcher acts like a portal sending your spirit to good dreams far away, but a solid one blocks passage in or out. So, I was inadvertently locking my spirit inside my bedroom every night. I complained to my dear daughter about having a recurring dream where I was looking down upon myself sleeping, but I never thought about it any more than that. When I died in my sleep in 1922, my spirit was permanently trapped.'

'I'm sure you could imagine how devastated I was, Mr. Richmond, when my father died,' Agatha says. 'I kept his room just as it was. Papa had been dead for two years, yet somehow, I still felt close to him, like I was talking to him in my dreams. Then, one night, the penny dropped. Something prompted me to remember a dream in which I was talking to my father on the opposite side of his bedroom door—he said he was trapped by the dreamcatcher. I removed the dreamcatcher from his door and left the gramophone playing before I went to sleep.'

Mr. Downing takes his daughter's hand and they start to dance. And as they do, Agatha says, 'That night, Mr. Richmond, two years after Papa's death, we were reunited, and we danced together. We have done so every night since, for over a hundred years now.' Agatha turns her gaze back to her father.

They dance their way into the centre of the room. Every movement is precise, their posture is perfect, and their speed is breath-taking. I marvel as I watch, and I feel glad. It is a dynamic display of what The Dream offers: it is a place where a daughter can forever dance with her father.

SLEEPING BEAUTY

I explore the different rooms of the downstairs party and meet more people. One minute I am lost in a deep philosophical conversation and the next I am howling with laughter. Everyone is excitable and charismatic and they tell fascinating stories, but most of all, they are welcoming. It is interesting to hear people's reasons for being here. To many, The Dream was a way to escape the real world, be it due to the Great Depression, the Second World War or the destruction of music by Rock 'n' Roll and The Beatles. They all make it clear that this house has become a place where kindred spirits not only relive but outlive. As the clock chimes for 4 a.m., the weight of the decision grows heavy on my shoulders.

I still don't understand how this all works. I find Agatha in the hallway. 'What happens if I don't ring the windchimes?' I ask.

'Then you will stay. Did you arrange for a wake-up call?'

'Yes, at 6 a.m.'

'Very well. A spirit must make their decision either before your wake-up call or by daylight, whichever is sooner. In this case, you must decide before 6 a.m.'

'Why, what happens at daylight?'

'Spirits do not like sunlight. It's why people wake up when it gets too bright. As for us, we go to our rooms at sunrise. The drapes are always closed.'

'Your rooms?'

'Yes, everyone who arrived before 1959 has their own room. We reached capacity in the private rooms that year but everyone gets a bed in which to dream. The two rooms in the attic on the northern side are for hosts and the two on the southern side are for guests. Mr. Richmond, if you wish to wake up, you must return to your room before 6 a.m. Otherwise, you may come into my room and we shall dance all day.'

'Which room is yours?'

'It is the first on the left at the top of the staircase. It is the one below yours.'

'But won't I wake when Mr. Baylor knocks on my door?'

'Mr. Baylor will assume that you have made your decision and place a dreamcatcher on your door, then he will knock. If your spirit is in your room, you will wake, but if your spirit is not inside, you will not wake—you will never wake. Instead, you will be immortal, and we will celebrate that every night.'

'Why won't I be able to wake?'

'It is like starting a fire, Mr. Richmond.'

'I don't understand.'

'You need oxygen, heat and fuel. Yes?'

'Yes.'

'Waking up is similar. You require a spark, some disturbance or stimulation, think of this as the heat and fuel. But you also need oxygen, this is the spirit. Without oxygen, there is no fire, and if your body is starved of its spirit, you cannot wake. You must decide before Mr. Baylor puts the dreamcatcher on your door and locks your spirit inside or out. And Mr. Richmond, I must stress that tonight is your only opportunity to join The Dream. People begin to remember their dreams when they reoccur.'

I pause for thought. I have less than two hours to decide whether to end my life and start anew. I wish I had longer. This place is wonderful, but while I will live forever, I am confined and restricted to these walls. But what is my life? Most of my days are working, and then I mostly like to sleep in on my days off. My friends and family are not the most exciting bunch, but everyone here is full of energy and they share my interests and intellect. These people are so hard to find in real life, yet I could make this my new family. Well, the Baylors don't exactly have much charisma, but they seem to be the exception.

'Who are the Baylors?' I ask. 'Are they your descendants?'

'Once I discovered The Dream, I lost my earthly desires, and without any children, I bequeathed my house to Mrs. Baylor's mother, a close and trusted friend who is here now. Whilst the Baylors may host The Dream, I retain the final decision. Had I beeped the telegraph twice, Mrs. Baylor would have placed a dreamcatcher on your door then and there. Your spirit would have been confined to your room.'

'And the gramophone—' I say, 'why didn't I hear its music when I woke up? This house is so quiet and noise travels so easily.'

'We spirits are sensitive to the forces of the earthly realm. The sun burns and so does the fire, but moonlight and smouldering embers warm us pleasantly. Sound is much the same as heat, what corporeal and ethereal beings can tolerate is not one and the same. I like a quiet house and Mrs. Baylor knows to speak softly. Therefore, Mr. Richmond, the gramophone has been adjusted to play at the lowest possible volume. It is tuned to be easily audible to us spirits rather than corporeal beings.'

I find the details fascinating, but there is no time to study this new realm. 'Miss Downing,' I say, 'I am truly grateful for the invite and this is a wonderful creation, but may I have a moment in my room to think the choice over?'

'Of course, Mr. Richmond. But make your decision by 6 a.m.'

'I will, thank you.'

I walk up to the curtain at the bottom of the stairs and stop. I stare at the painting on the wall. There are close to eighty people in the picture, and I recognise most of them now.

'Mrs. Baylor will paint you in too, Mr. Richmond,' Agatha says, before returning to dance in the ballroom.

This has been the most fun I have ever had. Coming here has been the lucky break that I never thought I would get. The people are fascinating and cultured and from generations past, present, and one day, future. And it is so in tune with my interests. History does not die here; jazz lives on and on. In just one night, I have discovered that I love to dance. What will I learn about myself tomorrow? I do not need a body to grow as a person. The Dream is like love at first sight, but knowing you must marry by the morning. I never thought I could be capable of something so rash, but I think I am. In fact, I'm sure I am.

Brimming with excitement, I walk through the curtain without opening it. I test again how it is that I can pass through objects without disturbing them. I am a ghost, but we are all ghosts when we dream. It makes a little sense now I think about it—you don't feel things when you dream. I don't recall ever opening a door in my dreams or eating food or suffering exhaustion. I have always loved sleeping, why not sleep forever?

I climb the marble stairs. Past the clutter at the top, I see the door to Agatha's room. I'm curious to see inside. I reach for the handle but my hand goes through. This is so surreal. I walk through the door.

Candles burn low and heavy curtains are drawn. A four-poster bed fills much of the room and its netting drapes are pulled closed. There are dolls and jewellery and other treasured possessions on show, which altogether is stylish. That is what Mrs. Baylor did before supper. She must have come in to dust and light candles so that Agatha can still enjoy her room as, I imagine, it has always been.

I approach the four-poster. The candlelight permeates through the netting. The bedsheets are dark and drape delicately over what appears to be someone slumbering underneath. My mind conjures the image of a sleeping beauty. Intrigue dares me to glance inside. It feels a little invasive, but Agatha did invite me to spend the day here. I approach the foot of the four-poster and feel my courage drain away. But curiosity fights courage. Whoever said "curiosity killed the cat" knew that curiosity always wins. I lean towards the netting and take a peek through.

I recoil from the bed with a breathless scream and cower in the corner. Agatha is still lying there—a skeleton.

The bones of her arms lie on top of grimy sheets and her fingerbones interleave where they meet. What was once beautiful golden hair is now bedraggled and dark red. Her skull stares vacantly through the ceiling as if Death is watching me where I sleep. And Death is grinning with one row of teeth, while the lower jaw rests like an ashtray ready to catch those not-so-pearly whites.

It appears that Agatha died as she slept, and her body has never been moved. The sheets that hang over the side of her bed are white, so their discolouration inside must be a result of decades of decay.

This room is a perverse shrine, and it occurs to me that all the rooms on this floor must be like this. Hawketh House is no guest house but rather a charnel house, where each room is a tomb honouring its dreamer. The type of person who chooses to enter

The Dream is like me—someone who is alone, unloved and unhappy. Therefore, this house is a mausoleum to dozens of sleeping beauties who never felt true love's first kiss.

THE COLD SPOT

I n Hawketh House, the dead still lie in their beds over a hundred years on. How badly must the house have reeked after someone died? That can't be a smell you get used to. Despite the grim reality, having a room preserved as you left it is a fitting memorial.

The party downstairs is not so loud from here, and I hear another noise—sobbing. I listen more carefully. It is coming from the upstairs. Agatha said the attic was for guests, and didn't Mrs. Baylor say that another guest stayed three nights ago? If she joined The Dream, I haven't met her yet.

I leave Agatha's room and weave my way through cluttered corridors towards the attic stairs. Each cluster of trinkets is localised around a single door, and each cluster is of a different style to the others. I presume, therefore, that the items pilled high outside each room are the earthly possessions of that room's occupier.

Passing door after door, the thought of each room containing a near-century-old corpse spooks me. The scale of death in this house is frightful. Can each room really contain a "sleeping beauty"? Once more, curiosity wins. I peer into one room and then another. Yes... Every room does indeed contain the skeletal remains of a dreamer. And each bed has become a rotten husk having had to absorb all the decomposing fluid matter of their occupiers. Truly disgusting.

I reach the attic stairs, and as I climb, the sobbing grows louder. A petite young woman in a silver dress sits curled up in a foetal position against the door opposite mine. She has long blonde hair that is held up with a claw clip. Her head is in her hands and she shakes as she sobs.

'Can I help you?' I say.

'Alastair!' she shouts. No one else here uses my first name. As she raises her head, I see that she has a small mole above her lip, and I vaguely recall seeing it before.

'What's the matter?' I ask as I squat down beside her. I put my hand on her shoulder, but she hits it away. She stares at me, trembling with rage. This isn't the first time a woman has been this angry with me and I haven't had a clue as to why. 'What did I do? And how do you know my name?'

'Why didn't you wake me up?'

'Wake you up...?'

'Al, you swore to me that you would wake yourself up and then come and wake me up. You woke yourself up all right with the windchimes and opened your door, then you just stared at me and went back inside.' She hits the door in anger, but it makes no sound. 'My body is dying in there! And I don't want to be here.'

'I didn't remember. I don't even remember your name now.'

'It's Rachael,' she says distastefully.

'Can you not get inside?' I ask. I too hit the door, but I feel nothing. I am completely numb.

'No! I can't! It's got one of these bloody dreamcatchers on it. The entire wall is unpassable.'

'I'm sorry, Rachael. But honestly, I had no memory. I heard the windchimes, panicked and then, thinking it was my imagination, I went back to sleep.'

'I can see that!' Rachael snaps.

I say nothing.

'You know, I thought you'd seen me at one point,' she says with sad resignation.

'You did?'

'Yeah, before you first went to bed. You were like feeling me somehow, obviously not touching me because your arm was passing through, but you seemed to sense my presence. You then got on your hands and knees and checked the floor.'

'The cold spot!'

'What?'

'I kept sensing a cold breath of air just there,' I say, pointing.

'Yeah, well, every time you came up, I was shouting at you, waving my arms, but each time you just passed through me. It was rude.'

'So it was a ghost.'

'Fuck you!'

'What?'

'Please don't call me a ghost. I'm having a hard time accepting my fate if you can't tell.'

'Sorry,' I say, timidly. 'I have to ask though, did you not choose to stay here?'

'Yes, I did.' Rachael groans. 'I was completely taken in by it. Christophe and I danced, and boy can he dance. For the first time in my life, I felt swept off my feet. There was a charm to this house that I didn't want to lose. It made the real world seem dull and plain. But I have quickly come to realise that it is a repetitive existence. I am only twenty-five, Al. There is so much more to see of the world. I want to live, travel, have children. I have sixty-odd years to feel things and taste food and listen to something other than fucking jazz.

Maybe when I'm eighty-five and my knees are shot, I'll put some dreamcatchers up in my own house, but not while I'm young.'

'Did you tell Agatha and the others?'

'Yes, but they can't understand why I'd want to wake up. I tried using Morse code on that thing last night. I have no idea what SOS sounds like, and Mrs. Baylor just looked on as dumb as a dopey dog.'

'I'm so sorry.' There's a long pause; I don't know how to help or comfort her. She is trapped. 'I'm afraid I don't know what SOS sounds like either.'

'I know you don't!' Rachael shouts. 'We've had this conversation before.' Rachael huffs, and after a pause, she says, 'I'm done for. Three nights my body has been inside there. I might be dead already; I have no way of telling.'

'I could try again, take down the dreamcatcher and wake you up.'

'You'll just forget again,' she says forlornly. 'And even if you were to remember, the door's locked. It's hope-less.'

We sit in silence. I can't help but feel responsible. Rachael's life depends on me waking up and remembering. If I wake up, it means I can't join, but Rachael has an excellent argument. This place is just a recurring dream, I have forty to fifty more years to live myself.

Rachael starts crying again and I just sit there, watching, listening, helpless. This poor girl wants to live, but what can I do? Do I really want to wake up? It's not like I haven't realised the consequences. I'm not in a position where I have loads of money to travel and have fun. My life is a struggle. Do I really want to go back to it? Can I live with myself if I stay, though? Rachael will be unhappy forever, and forever is a long time to resent me for my failure to help her. If I do nothing, I might as well have murdered this poor girl.

I contemplate my predicament over and over, then one of the attic clocks chimes quietly five times. Make a decision man! I leave Rachael crying and walk towards my room, still not knowing if I'm going to ring the windchimes or not. If I wake up now, there is no chance of me getting back to sleep in time, and even if I did, I still wouldn't remember The Dream. Agatha would have to explain it all over again.

I enter my room, and I panic at the sight of me. I stand over my sleeping body. This is fucking surreal! My mouth is open and drooling on the pillow; I'm no sleeping beauty. I think about what will happen to my body if I don't wake up. It will most likely die gasping for water; how many days that'll be, I don't know. Mrs. Baylor will then move my corpse to a bed somewhere, but Agatha said the room would not be private, so I can expect gawping eye sockets from long-dead dreamers to leer jealously upon my white opals. Death will suck out my eyes, and I will don the guise of His eternal creed.

I think of my family and how their hearts will break. They will wonder endlessly why I disappeared. If my sister went missing, I would never cease searching for her, and I know she'll do the same for me. The thought of their anguish terrifies me.

I rush towards the windchimes and hit them as hard as I possibly can.

DÉJÀ VU

'Who's there?' I shout, pointing my penknife at the darkness. The windchimes are jangling—again! This isn't a dream. I flick the light on—nobody! The windchimes dance, but there's no one here. 'Who did that?' I call out. There is no response.

This is a practical joke. Mrs. Baylor has rigged them to go off to make me think this house is haunted. It is utter nonsense to believe in ghosts. She is trying to get a reaction from me. Is she filming?

'Very funny,' I say to any hidden cameras. I put the penknife down to prove to anyone who might watch that I'm not scared.

I get up to inspect the windchimes. I take them off the hook and scrutinise the beam and the windchimes. Fuck! They're not rigged. There is nothing that could have set them off. I ask the unthinkable: do ghosts exist?

The key is still in the door; it hasn't moved. No one has come into my room. I check again for a draught—nothing. I open a window; the night air is still. There is no chance of any strong winds tonight. I pull out the bed to check under it—why, I don't know—there is nothing.

I open the door. The landing is empty, besides the clutter. The house is so quiet that I can hear my heart pounding. Something is going on. I bet I'll find Mrs. Baylor sniggering if I go downstairs. I grab my robe from inside and take the key from the door, being sure to lock it behind me.

There's that icy chill again! What is it with this spot? I tiptoe down the attic stairs, but against the silence, the house roars like a lion.

I look over the bannister at the top of the marble stairs and see the drapes at the bottom are closed, but the floor glows suggesting daylight on the other side. The windows, however, confirm it's still night. Mrs. Baylor must be hiding behind the drapes with the lights on.

I sneak down. Where the staircase turns, the red eyes of the rabbit figurine stare at me. The fish-head ornament makes me shudder, the sight of them brings a strange sense of déjà vu. I creep down the remaining stairs. Is Mrs. Baylor on the other side of the curtain? If she is, I think I might thump the crazed bitch. I'll take a laugh at her expense. Anger sears through me. I want to startle her and make her scream. I whip open the drapes.

I stare, stunned. Dozens of candles flicker in the gust I create opening the curtain. The hallway is empty; Mrs. Baylor is nowhere to be seen. I look at *The Dream* painting and then I enter the ballroom. The large space bathes in candlelight and moonlight. The strange thing is that this is not unexpected. The sense of déjà vu is powerful, almost to the point I feel I can predict what might happen next.

I stand quietly for a moment while I think, but I get a sudden chill. It's the same icy draught as in the attic, but unlike the attic, it passes quickly. Then it comes again, and soon I am flushing hot and cold. Am I not well?

A whirring noise draws my attention along with a quiet voice, a woman's voice. It sounds like she is talking quietly in the kitchen.

'Hello?' I ask the empty room. Nothing changes. She continues to talk as if she hasn't heard me.

I find the source of the whirring: the gramophone is spinning. I walk to it; the voice grows louder. I lift the needle. It moves very easily; it must be well-oiled. Her talking stops.

'Hello?' I ask again, thinking she may have heard me. There is no response.

Why is the gramophone spinning, and why isn't it playing? I replace the needle on the record. The voice returns. I reach into the gramophone's shiny brass speaker, and as I pull out fistfuls of socks, the gramophone comes to life. Reality and déjà vu snap together and become one. My eyes grow wide...

Ruth Etting sings as I freeze in terror, feeling the eyes of ghosts upon me.

My body tingles. I'm too petrified to turn around. What will I see? It was a dream! How can it be real? But it is—I know it is.

I stand still and gawp at the spinning record. I don't want to confirm it; they are looking at me. I am standing both in the 2020s and the 1920s. The party is happening around me. This house keeps more than their memories alive.

Every single night we humans enter this dream world, yet we remain blind and stupid. We perceive its existence yet disregard it as a flight of fancy. We charge those who understand or act on their dreams as being charlatans or madmen, but it is our minds that have yet to open. I have attained madman's knowledge, and I understand that the dream and the house are one. Death is not a demon; it is like a snake shedding its skin. I feel the eyes from the other world upon me. They peer over my shoulder, and I feel their cold presence. Their lives spin and spin like the record; my life is like a cassette—one day it will run to the end and stop.

I turn slowly to face the new reality. I see it—now that I know what to look for—I see it. The ballroom is a dancing shimmer. A haze fills it like carbon monoxide, invisible and deadly. The room seems to slowly sway and the ground swells like the ocean. My sea legs quake and I fall. I tremble on the floor, and still the room shifts and heaves and hauls. I realise that the subtle distortions of lights are from the spirits of dreamers, and now with so many overlapping, the effect is amplified such that I am dizzy.

I recollect my waltz with a beautiful flapper girl—Agatha, that was her name. I remember her offer to relive the Roaring Twenties within this dream-house forever. I understand that the first floor is reserved for sleeping beauties and the attic is for new guests. Then I recall the cold spot and the pitiful crying girl—Rachael!

I remember now why I woke—I must save Rachael. I rush out of the ballroom. The hallway shimmers, another room full of ghosts. I dart towards the stairs, but I pause... Rachael said her door was locked. In this house, the sound of breaking her door would surely alert the Baylors. No, Mrs. Baylor will have a spare set of keys or perhaps even a master key somewhere. I stay downstairs and search desperately for keys. The hooks, the drawers, the cupboards—no keys.

I race from one room to another in my frantic hunt, then as I turn on a rug, it slides out from under me. I land with a hollow thump on a polished wooden floor. A sharp pain cuts my hip, and I curse as I climb back to my feet. A metal ring-handle gleams where my hip landed, and I spy a square-shaped edge in the shiny floor. The rug was hiding this... Could it be a trapdoor? I reach down, grasp the ring-handle, and pull up.

The door in the floor opens, revealing a set of stone steps into a dark void below. What could be down there? And might I find the keys? It would certainly be a good place to hide them.

The trapdoor is hinged, and I quietly set it down with the door open. Candles fill all the downstairs rooms, and I grab a candlestick with four candles. I stare down into the blackness, but then I snap myself out of it—I don't have time for fear.

Cold, rough stone prickles my bare feet as I take my first steps down. I should not be entering an unknown underground space in just a nightrobe, but I press on. My pace is slow but my heart rate quickens. With each step down, the speed and volume of my thumping chest ratchets up. It's as though my heart is tethered to the ground and every step down pulls on a straining cord.

The candles that guide my descent illuminate bare stone walls, and then, emerging from the darkness ahead is a black door. My fingers tingle, my head spins, and my feet quake. My body protests, but I descend further. Then as I grasp the handle of the black door, I cry out in pain as hot wax from one of the candles lands on my bare foot. My tender skin burns, and I hop around, frantically trying to brush it off with my robe.

I compose myself and cast a wistful glance up the stairs to the bright opening above. Swallowing my reservations, I turn back to face the black door, twist the handle, and, with a heavy push, it opens.

THE NIGHTMARE
BENEATH THE DREAM

A foetid stench fills my nose as I push open the heavy black door to the basement. Its acrid potency stings my eyes. Tall, lit candles stand in gloopy masses of wax that drip down their ledges and feed waxy mounds below. The floor shimmers dankly, and the walls glisten in grime. It's a large, dismal space. My eyes take a moment to adjust to the gloom, but what they slowly resolve is darkly hideous.

My bare foot squelches in some horrid, goopy mess as I step inside. A new and overpowering stench hits me, causing me to retch. I look down at the floor, but I can't make out what I've stepped in. It's a layer of black grime with strings of colours—reds, whites and purples. I grimace as I take a few steps further. With each step is a squelch, and then my foot slips, and I barely catch my balance. I do not want to fall in this! I find sliding my feet through the squalid mess helps me maintain my balance.

Beside me is a sideboard; why it's down here, I'm not sure. Its drawers are stiff, but I open them in search of keys. A glittery sparkle of jewellery greets me as I search each one, but I find no keys. I pass the sideboard and then a bookcase, and much more of the room comes into view. My mouth drops open as I gawp around. The scale is staggering. Another wave of rancid smells triggers me to retch once more.

Candles illuminate the entire vault with their meagre lustre, and I gawp across row upon row of four-poster beds. Each one has a black mattress, black netting, black sheets... black everything. This blackened bedroom stretches across the entire footprint of the house—it's gigantic!

Each bed has its own surrounding space, with large furniture—tables, sideboards, bookcases and sofas—lining the perimeter, effectively creating a makeshift bedroom. These items are all black too. And I can be sure that everything wasn't black to begin with; rather, years wallowing in such a squalid environment has stained it all in the same grime that coats the walls and the floors.

Much like how the furniture lining the corridors on the first floor match with the adjacent room, the style of the furniture down here also matches these makeshift bedrooms. Trinkets and antiques stand on the furniture too, and this also mimics the first floor as the style changes as you go from one room to the next. The perimeter items and furniture do not reach much past shoulder height, so I see all the makeshift bedrooms that the gloom will allow. Each one has a few candles, and it is enough to illuminate the shadowy figure of a "sleeping beauty" lying in each bed.

I shuffle down a narrow passageway—a makeshift corridor—to a gap in the furniture, which acts like a doorway to the first of these bedrooms. My feet brush past miscellaneous items, some hard, some slimy. I try not to think about what they might be. Gazing upon this room's sleeping beauty, I wonder which dreamer this might be.

I move to the next makeshift bedroom, but, peering through the entrance, I put my hands over my mouth and swallow a scream. The bed has partially collapsed. It's split down the middle on the near side. A skull remains at the head of the bed but bones and dried remnants of rotten flesh lie in a clump at the base. I heave and turn away, looking at my feet. However, now

I can see better what it is that I'm standing it. As the cadavers have decayed over decades, their rotting entrails and fluids have leaked through frayed or broken mattresses and spilt onto the floor. I'm standing in a slop of corpse juice!

I glance at the door I came in and spy a pair of Wellington Boots. Why have I only just seen them now? Mrs. Baylor must come in to light the candles, but given the tall height of the candles and the size of their wax beds, it's a job she must do rarely. I don't blame her for not wanting to enter this cesspit, but why is it like this at all?

This basement is a dark mirror of the first floor, which is merely a freakshow in comparison to this ghastly opus of horror. It is a nightmare beneath the dream. Mrs. Baylor regularly enters and cleans the first floor; she would have removed much of the corpse leakage over the years, and she could open a window too. As basements are naturally damp with no ventilation, I can imagine this bedroom crypt deteriorating rapidly.

This vault is a vast ossuary reflecting the corporeal reality of the decisions made by the dreamers. Agatha said that everyone before '59 had a private room in the house; she neglected to mention that this is where everyone has come since. I lift my head and scan. It's frightful gazing over so many rows of blackened four-poster beds stretching through the gloom, each one representing a dead dreamer.

A few rows across, I spy a bed where the cadaver inside bloats. This is no skeleton—the cadaver is in active decay. Gagging, I look away.

The netting of the two adjacent beds is drawn open and there are no sleeping beauties inside. There's no candles or furniture either. These two are likely ear-marked for Rachael and me if I don't hurry. My stomach churns at the prospect of being lain to rot in one of these "dream" beds. Beyond these two beds is a patch of darkness, where all I can resolve are more empty beds awaiting future dreamers.

There's no way the Baylors regularly come down here to collect keys. I'm wasting time. I must act now to save Rachael lest she end up here.

I wade back through the foul remnants of rotten carcasses. I continue retching, but my stomach remains strong. Pulling the heavy black door closed behind me, I gratefully inhale fresh air. I climb back up to the ground floor, wipe the grime off my feet with a nearby cloth, close the trapdoor, and replace the rug.

I race back through the hallway and up the stairs. The house snarls. It has captured Rachael in its dream. I reach her room and tear the dreamcatcher off the door. I stare at the bare wood where the dreamcatcher stood. Has it worked? Will Rachael wake up? I put my ear to her door and listen.

AT DEATH'S DOOR

Weak gasps stir inside Rachael's room when all was silent before. I try Rachael's door and confirm that it's locked. Her hoarse gasps continue, coarse as sandpaper. A thump triggers a whimper. I throw my shoulder into the door, but I bounce off. The house is built to be sturdy even if it does noisily complain. I kick and kick the door. Not only am I sounding an alarm call for the Baylors, but the door barely yields. This stubborn barrier may decide the fate of Rachael and me.

I run up and charge with my shoulder. The door creaks but does not give way. I attack again, and the wooden frame groans. And again. And again, until the door bursts open with a deafening crack, and I crash through onto the floor inside.

I jump to my feet as a foul odour burns my nostrils. A gaunt girl in a nightdress flaps frantically on the floor beside a bed, which has been soiled. I rush to Rachael; her eyes plead for help. She is clutching her throat, which grates like rusty cogs as she tries to swallow. Her muscles protrude as they stretch dry and taught skin. Brown eyes continue to beg—she's so dehydrated that she seems unable to speak.

My eyes sweep the room. I rush to the sink and run the tap at full speed, splashing water everywhere. I fill a cup and race back to Rachael. She clutches the glass like a baby clings to a bottle.

She drinks and drinks, each swallow oils the cogs. She hands me back the glass, empty. I quickly refill it and return it to her. I also grab some biscuits from the side. Rachael snatches them out of my hand and eats them like a greedy peasant. She then drinks some more and squeezes my hand. It is a thank you. This young woman was at death's door.

'Mr. Richmond, what is the matter?' Mrs. Baylor shouts up from downstairs.

Shit! Mrs. Baylor won't let us leave if we remember The Dream.

I recall Geoffrey, *the man who woke up*. His fate was to return to The Dream, but how did he go from alive and awake to dead and dreaming? Was it against his will? Did Mrs. Baylor kill him? Will she kill us too to keep the secret within these walls? Rachael's door is wide open. I must stop her before she comes up.

I race out of the room and down the steep attic steps. Mrs. Baylor confronts me at the bottom, standing arms crossed in a purple robe and her dark hair resting loose. The landing light is on, and she squints as if the brightness hurts her tired eyes. 'Mr. Richmond, what is the matter?' she says again, flatly.

'I'm so sorry to disturb you. I woke in a panic. The windchimes in the room were jangling. I couldn't make out what caused it.'

'A draught, Mr. Richmond.'

'It must have been.' I wipe my sweaty hands on my robes and feel my heart thumping.

'Have you been in the dining room, Mr. Richmond? The gramophone was playing loudly.'

'Oh.' Shit! What do I say? 'I—I—' I freeze as though there is a great spotlight upon me. 'I had some silly thought that there might be a ghost in my room, so I wanted to leave. I went downstairs and saw the record spinning and noticed there were socks inside. The music helped calm me down.'

'I forgot to turn it off, Mr. Richmond. What was the banging upstairs?'

'I thought I'd lost my keys, so I was frantically searching all the cupboards.'

'Did you find them?'

'Yes, Mrs. Baylor.' Please believe me and go back to bed.

'And there was nothing else...?' Mrs. Baylor's tired eyes open a little wider.

'No, just the keys.'

'Very well. It is quarter past five, Mr. Richmond. Would you still like a wake-up call, or would you prefer an earlier breakfast?'

'No, 7 a.m. is fine for breakfast, but I will stay awake now, so Mr. Baylor won't need to come up to the attic.'

'As you wish, Mr. Richmond. I will see you for breakfast.' Mrs. Baylor turns and disappears through the corridors.

I breathe out, relieved. I think she believed me. I still have a massive problem though, how do I get Rachael out of here? I could have breakfast as normal and leave with Mrs. Baylor thinking I don't remember my dream, but if she sees that I have woken Rachael, she will know, and she will try to kill us both. I creep back upstairs, vowing to keep the noise down.

I enter Rachael's room. God! It stinks. It doesn't compare to the near-toxic crypt, but it's gross nonetheless. I shut the door behind me. I don't want the smell to find Mrs. Baylor. Rachael is sat up eating biscuits. 'Can I get you another drink?' I ask.

'Yes, please.' Her words grate in her throat. I pour another glass and return to her. 'I feel like I know you. Is your name Alastair?'

'It is.'

'Where am I, Al?'

'We're in Hawketh House.'

'What's wrong with me? I feel like I've been hallucinating. Am I ill?'

'Not now you're not. You have been dreaming for three days, unable to wake up.'

'Three days... dreaming...' The realisation spreads across her face.

She remembers The Dream, and I fill in the gaps in her memory. Soon, her face turns from realisation to fear.

'Mrs. Baylor,' Rachael starts, 'she won't let us leave, will she?'

'No, we have to find a way to get out of here.'

'The window?' she says, looking over my shoulder.

'Too high, and you are very weak.'

'Weak?' Rachael scoffs. She tries to lift herself off the floor and onto the bed, but she slips and crumples back down. 'I think my legs are still asleep,' she says with a weak smile. I help her up onto the bed.

'I'll get us out of here. Either we find a key to the front door, or we break one of the windows downstairs.'

'Okay,' she says.

'We cannot leave dressed like this. We need to change.'

'Would you hold onto me a moment, Al? I want to try and stand up.'

Rachael puts her arm over my shoulder and lifts herself off the bed. 'I can't believe this. I'm a fucking walking corpse. If you were just a few moments later, I think—I think I'd be dead.'

I support her as she walks to the wardrobe, and I help her gather her clothes. 'Can I come to your room, Al? It's fucking foul in here.'

'Of course.' I help her across the landing. She walks ever so slowly. When she finally slumps on my bed, she sighs loudly and says, 'Thank you.'

'It's no trouble,' I say. I grab my clothes. 'Are you able to change? I'll go to the bathroom to give you some privacy.'

Rachael grins. 'This is no time to be prudish. Can we save the embarrassment for when we escape?'

'*If* we escape.'

'You are strong Alastair, and they are old. They won't think twice about killing us, so you shouldn't fret about killing them. If you don't hesitate, we will get away. My life is in your hands; I trust you.' I can only muster a weak smile.

As I get dressed, Rachael's words swirl through my head. *You shouldn't fret about killing them*. I haven't thought about attacking them. I want to escape before the Baylors even know we've gone.

I help Rachael out of her soiled nightie and into a clean hoody and jeans. As I do so, she grasps me with grateful touches. It is endearing. No one has ever depended on me before. It triggers a surge of courage, and I snatch my penknife.

'You're going to need something bigger than that,' Rachael says.

'I should be able to get a knife from the kitchen.'

The only correct clock ticks past five-thirty as we prepare our escape. We have less than half an hour before the Baylors get up. I have my rucksack on my back with anything that we might need. I plan to simply run for the hills, carrying Rachael until I can get a phone signal to call the police. There's also a chance of flagging down a car, but there won't be much traffic at this hour. Before all that though, I've got to get us out of this house.

'Rachael, let me carry you down the stairs. You're walking better now, but I don't want Mrs. Baylor to hear two sets of footsteps. This house is an audible map, everyone knows where everyone is.'

She agrees, and as we leave my room, I give her a fireman's lift. The house creaks exceptionally loudly under both of our weights. The steep attic stairs are particularly difficult to navigate. I face forward and Rachael helps us balance by grasping the steps as we go down. The first-floor landing is empty, and I creep as quietly as possible. As yet, no one else stirs. I would hear the Baylors. Descending the marble stairs, I see the drapes remain pulled across. Is the gala still happening?

At the bottom, I drop Rachael to her feet. I mouth, 'Are you okay?' She nods. 'Help me find the front door key and the car keys,' I whisper. 'I searched the drawers in the hallway earlier, let's try the dining room.' Rachael agrees, and in her eagerness, she is the first through the drapes.

The temperature plummets and my sea legs return. The spirits are still here but now there's no music. I try not to think about them, but I glance at the happy faces in the painting. Did I make the right decision? Rachael then looks back at me with hope in her big, brown eyes. Yes, I have.

We enter the ballroom and search a few drawers.

BEEP! BEEP! BEEP! BEEP! BEEP! BEEP! BEEP! BEEP! BEEP! BEEP! BEEP!

The telegraph is going mad. Hope washes from Rachael's face. Agatha is trying to alert Mrs. Baylor. I grab the telegraph machine and tear it from the wall. It falls silent.

Rachael and I breathe a sigh of relief.

Something catches my eye. The arm of the gramophone is moving all by itself, then the speaker blares into life at full volume: 'Ten cents a dan—'

I rip out the record. The gramophone falls silent.

There's a creak on the stairs.

Mrs. Baylor has heard us.

LIVE AND LET LIVE

R achael and I share a wide-eyed stare, startled by the sound of Mrs. Baylor descending towards us. 'Grab the knives,' Rachael whispers in panic.

I rush into the kitchen and frantically rummage through the drawers. Two chef's knives gleam. I grab them, discarding my penknife. The house moans, and I track the footsteps above. Rachael is waiting at the dining room door, her eyes full of terror. I thrust the handle of one of the knives into her hand.

'Try and break the window with the handle,' I say. 'I'll guard you.'

Rachael staggers over as fast as she can, but she is moving better. The window might be our only way to escape. I will do everything to make sure Rachael and I get out but attacking the Baylors is a last resort.

The house's loud warning subsides and footsteps echo. I stand a few metres from the hallway door. I train the knife on the entrance and adopt a fighting stance. I am ready to pounce.

'Break it!' I shout to Rachael at the window.

Rachael thumps the glass, but it holds firm.

A flash of purple, and Mrs. Baylor leers from the doorway.

Rachael hits the glass again.

'DON'T...' Mrs. Baylor's sharp cry stuns us. She lets the warning hang, then calmly adds, '...do that, Miss Mountford.'

'Stay ba—' I start.

'Mr. Richmond, Miss Mountford,' Mrs. Baylor cuts me off. 'You wish to leave this house, correct?' Rachael and I share a nervous glance but say nothing. 'You both remember The Dream, correct?'

Rachael reacts, 'Let us out, you old witch!'

'Miss Mountford, I hold no one in this house against their will. You do not need to break the windows to leave. And Mr. Richmond, lower the knife, please. I don't know what threat you think an old woman poses.' Mrs. Baylor's tone is unnervingly calm and such confidence worries me. I hold the knife firm. 'But

Miss Mountford, you must be so desperately hungry. Would you both stay for breakfast?'

'You don't fool us, Mrs. Baylor,' Rachael snaps. 'Why would you let us leave? The secret will get out.'

'I would like to discuss that little matter with you over breakfast, if I may.'

'Tell us now,' Rachael says.

'Miss Mountford, no one will believe your ghost story, but I wish for us to agree a truce, whereby you protect our secret. Live and let live, don't you think?' Neither me nor Rachael answer. 'Of course, there is another option. Mr. Richmond, Miss Mountford, until you leave this house, the offer to join The Dream remains.'

'Piss off, Mrs. Baylor,' Rachael bites back. 'I nearly died because of you. This place is a recurring nightmare; you ain't gonna convince me to stay.'

'Very well, I shall ask Mr. Baylor to provide breakfast before you leave, and we can discuss the terms of our truce.' Rachael and I look at each other, unsure whether to accept. 'Mr. Baylor!' Mrs. Baylor shouts upstairs, then she commands, 'Everybody out. Except you two, of course.' The shimmery haze disappears, and the room warms; the ghosts are returning to their rooms.

Mrs. Baylor walks up to me and my knife. She puts her hand softly on mine and gently pushes down. 'Please, Mr. Richmond. Live and let live.'

I lower the knife.

Mrs. Baylor pulls a table into the room, places a tablecloth and candle on top and draws up three chairs. 'Mr. Richmond, Miss Mountford, please take a seat. Mr. Baylor will get us breakfast and coffee while we discuss, then Mr. Baylor will drive you both to the station.'

The house alerts us to Mr. Baylor's arrival. He is met by Mrs. Baylor, but when Mr. Baylor sees Rachael, he staggers backwards in shock.

'It is quite all right, dear,' Mrs. Baylor says. 'They remember The Dream. I will join them for breakfast and make my peace offering. Would you kindly make up three breakfasts and three of our house-blend coffees please, dear?'

Mr. Baylor nods and grunts once. Mrs. Baylor turns towards us, but as Mr. Baylor walks to the kitchen, his glance flits between Rachael and me. The man is physically shaking—he looks terrified. I think he's scared that exposing the secret of dead bodies in bedrooms and an underground ossuary will bring the authorities to Hawketh House. They will go to prison for life and The Dream will die.

'Won't you join me?' Mrs. Baylor says, sitting at the table.

I want to live and let live. I have no desire to end The Dream, especially if her promise to let us leave is truthful. Either way, if I do not sit, I will be forced into conflict with the Baylors. I join her at the table.

'Alastair! How dare you take her side!' Rachael shouts.

'Rachael, you need to eat. Live and let live.'

'Live and let LIVE?' Rachael cries. 'This witch left me for DEAD!' Rachael stumbles back and clatters into the window. Her knife drops to the floor. She has grown faint, likely as a result of her rage, but she catches her fall and leans on the windowsill. I rush to her, put her arm over my shoulder and hold her up.

'You're absolutely exhausted, Rachael,' I say. 'You need food. Let Mr. Baylor bring us breakfast.'

'Protect me, Al,' Rachael says softly. 'I don't trust her. Keep hold of the knife.'

'Yes, I will.'

Mrs. Baylor gets up to assist. 'Please, Mrs. Baylor, stay seated,' I say. 'You have not earned our trust. I will look after Rachael.'

'Very well, Mr. Richmond. Breakfast and coffee will revive her.'

'What's this house-blend coffee?' I ask as I prop Rachael in the seat. She holds her balance as if she's coming around. I sit down but keep hold of the knife under the table.

'It is a blend which we have perfected over many years. It's black coffee with an infusion of hazelnut and almonds.'

I am only half-listening as I'm desperately worried about Rachael. She's drifting through waves of consciousness and semi-consciousness; one moment she is looking at me, then the next her eyes start rolling. I thought she was out of the woods, but now I'm not so sure. 'Do you need an ambulance?' I ask Rachael.

'The nearest phone box is a mile away,' Mrs. Baylor cuts in. 'Rachael has been sleeping for three days; her body is weak, but food and drink will bring her around, Mr. Richmond.'

Mr. Baylor walks in with a tray of coffees. The saucers rattle—he is still shaking. The chattering of china grows louder as he lowers the tray to the table, and then it lands with a crash. Rachael jolts back into alertness, yet somehow, the coffees don't spill.

'Steady, dear,' Mrs. Baylor says.

Mr. Baylor carefully selects a coffee, the cup and saucer rattle once more as he lifts it over the others and then places it in front of his wife. He clatters a coffee in front of Rachael then spills a bit as he delivers mine.

'Don't worry, dear,' Mrs. Baylor says. 'We will come to an agreement. The Dream will not end.'

'It bloody should,' Rachael says as Mr. Baylor exits.

'Live and let live,' Mrs. Baylor repeats.

No one responds. The silence is only broken by bursts of breath to cool the hot coffee.

'What is your offer, Mrs. Baylor?' I ask.

'After food, Mr. Richmond. Miss Mountford needs to recover somewhat first.'

'I'm fine!' Rachael bites. Neither Mrs. Baylor nor I are convinced.

'Coffee shouldn't be too hot now,' Mrs. Baylor says. 'I hope you like our blend. We've never had a bad review.' As a way to encourage us, Mrs. Baylor takes a sip. I lift my cup. The aroma of fresh coffee is comforting.

Rachael takes a sip.

I take a sip. It tastes bitter.

Mrs. Baylor drinks.

Rachael drinks.

I drink.

We keep drinking the bitter coffee.

LIVE AND LET DIE

After sipping our coffees, there comes a violent coughing and choking. Mrs. Baylor clutches her throat. Mr. Baylor comes rushing in. He grabs his wife's flailing arms and grasps her hands tightly. Mrs. Baylor's eyes stare widely, charging her husband. Mr. Baylor blubbers and mumbles. I think he is repeating, 'Forgive me,' over and over.

I spit my coffee on the floor and throw Rachael's away, but Rachael and I have drunk just as much as our hostess.

Mrs. Baylor's chokes transform into the gurgles of an undead corpse. White foam froths from her mouth. Her eyes roll. Her whole head lurches to the side and then tips back. White eyes stare to the heavens as her body convulses like someone possessed by a demon. Mr. Baylor is bawling into her lap. The man is distraught. Rachael and I remain fine. Was it a mistake? Was the poisoned coffee meant for us?

The violent theatre ends and white foam drools out Mrs. Baylor's mouth and down her neck. She is dead. I grasp Rachael's hand to comfort her. She squeezes it hard. Not only is the site of drool sliding like a slug horrid, but we can both be quite sure that Mrs. Baylor intended the poisoned coffee for us.

Mr. Baylor continues to weep, but an alarm goes off in the kitchen.

'You meant to poison us!' I charge, pulling out my knife.

The distraught man shakes his head and grunts twice.

'You cannot expect me to believe you poisoned your wife.'

Mr. Baylor howls in despair, but then nods and grunts once. The kitchen alarm is frantic, but Mr. Baylor is clutching his wife too tightly to care. If Mr. Baylor had, indeed, meant to poison Rachael and I, surely, he would have poisoned two cups, not one.

The alarm in the kitchen screeches like an enraged animal. I am not just going to sit here; Rachael needs food and then we need to get out of this madhouse. I grab Rachael's arm, hold it over my shoulder and hoist her up as I stand. We stagger to the kitchen, leaving Mr. Baylor to mourn.

Smoke greets us as I open the door, and I hurry to the far side. I rest Rachael on a stool, where she slumps against the counter, and then I take a frying pan with charcoal bacon off the hob. I go from one window to another until a small window up high opens. The smoke is not thick enough to choke, but the siren deafens and frightens. I grab a rolling pin and bash the ceiling-mounted alarm until it falls silent. Rachael slips and falls forward. I dash and catch her before she topples off the stool. She needs food!

The fridge is right beside us. I open it. There is plenty that Rachael can eat. When she sees this, her eyes flare, and she lunges towards the food like a vampire to an open blood vessel. As Rachael feasts and the smoke clears, I look behind and see a bright red coffee jar with two labels, both reading: "House Blend!" Presumably, it is labelled twice so no deadly mistakes are made if one label falls off.

Mr. Baylor's blubbering is the only sound besides Rachael's scoffing. Did he really mean to poison his wife? I can't think why he would do such a thing, but I still can't understand why only one cup was poisoned.

I look back to Rachael, who is chomping through a block of cheese when a large figure appears in my periphery and startles me. It's Mr. Baylor. He stops dead in the doorway and seems to panic too. Had he forgotten that we were here? Mr. Baylor then grabs a tea towel and hurries back out. I leave Rachael and peer through the doorway. I watch as Mr. Baylor closes his wife's eyes and mops up her drool. His actions are not those of a man who has made a terrible mistake but more akin to a man seeking forgiveness.

When I look back, Rachael is standing; already she is much stronger. This is good, now we can leave. Rachael comes to me. I urge her to be quiet, and then we creep behind Mr. Baylor and reach the hallway. The front door is still locked. Shit! How do we get out?

Rachael starts searching coat pockets and drawers for keys, but I've already searched to no avail. The only other place I can think to search is the Baylors' room. Breaking the windows has already proved difficult and it might antagonise Mr. Baylor. We could get a nasty cut from the broken glass too. No, I think it is best to appeal to Mr. Baylor.

I approach the big, blubbering man with Rachael hanging back. We both still have our knives should he decide to attack, but he is not currently posing a threat. Either he lets us out or we will force our way out, one way or another.

Mrs. Baylor only ever raised her voice when Rachael tried breaking the window; it makes me wonder if doing so might somehow break the house's spell and destroy The Dream... The Dream! Of course! Mrs. Baylor is not truly gone; she must live on in The Dream.

As I watch Mr. Baylor cradling his wife's body, I feel sure this was no accident. He is muttering an apology, which her spirit may be able to hear. She was always destined to join The Dream; she has just arrived sooner than planned.

'Mr. Baylor, is your wife alive in The Dream now?' I ask. 'Is that why you poisoned her coffee, because she is not really dead?'

He looks up tearfully and nods. He then grabs a notepad and pen and writes, *I agreed to be the housekeeper so long as a person's wishes were maintained, but my wife insisted that we keep some cyanide in case somebody should remember and a leak needed to be contained. The Dream is something special, but I see the death behind it. I refuse to enter the rooms and the basement. I hate the death and the possibility that I may be asked to administer it. 'House blend', you may have gathered, is our code for putting cyanide in a guest's drink.*

'Why did it taste so bad if you didn't poison ours?'

I squeezed some lemon in because you were expecting a house blend that would taste different. I added hazelnut to my wife's to sweeten the bitter almond taste of the poison. If blended well, it is tough to tell any difference.

'How do you know what cyanide tastes like?'

Mr. Baylor bows his head shamefully.

'Geoffrey,' I say, knowing that Mr. Baylor would speak to him in The Dream.

Mr. Baylor grunts once. He writes: *I couldn't kill another innocent person. Geoffrey was my fault, and it was for me to make amends. I have never seen my wife so angry. She made absolutely sure that it would never happen again. She corrected me.*

'Corrected you, how?'

Mr. Baylor opens his mouth and attempts to stick out his tongue. I wince at the sight of it. It looks like a swollen tonsil; his tongue must have been cut by a knife.

'That's barbaric!' I cry.

I deserved much worse. Geoffrey may be glad to be here, but I have never told him that his business went under and his family were bankrupted. It was all my fault, but it was a mistake I would not make again. That is why I did not poison your coffee. My wife is in The Dream now; she will live on, and I will see her there.

———◇———

The latches click and the front door creaks like a vault opening. I deeply breathe in the cool, crisp air. Lake Linketh stretches serenely for miles amongst a canvas of autumn that paints hope with its beauty.

There is joy in my heart as Rachael and I check out of Hawketh House. Mr. Baylor's actions to spare our lives at great personal expense convince Rachael and me to keep the secret of The Dream House. Grateful, Mr. Baylor offers to drive us to the station, and we accept. I am not afraid of a secret scheme or trap; Mr. Baylor is a timid, obedient man who seems very much lost without his wife's instruction.

Mr. Baylor opens the back seats to his Jaguar. Inside, Rachael grabs my hand, smiles, and mouths, 'Thank you.' She looks healthy now—and pretty too. The engine starts, and Hawketh House hides behind the trees as we drive away.

The feisty young lady holds my hand the whole journey. My heart leaps and bounds. I'm going to get back a day early, but maybe Rachael will want to spend the time with me.

A chorus of seagulls welcomes us to Skelgate and the train station. Mr. Baylor turns into the car park. 'Mr. Baylor,' I say, 'we cannot thank you enough. You have spared our lives and we promise to keep your secret.'

Mr. Baylor ratchets the handbrake and reaches into his coat pocket. He writes a note and hands it to me. It reads:

Mr. Richmond,

I request three things of you. Firstly, enjoy your life. Secondly, I must ask a favour: at 9 a.m. tomorrow go to a phone box and call the Deaconshire Constabulary. Say that your name is Mr. Baylor and that you have an urgent need for an officer to visit Hawketh House, then hang up. Finally, and most importantly, protect the secret and keep The Dream alive.

Yours sincerely,
Delbert Baylor

Following our ordeal, Rachael comes back to my house near Manchester, and we complete Mr. Baylor's request. A week on and Rachael is still here. We've become inseparable. It's been a wonderful week—I couldn't be happier.

Now, as we're snuggling together and watching a film, there comes a heavy knock at the front door. I answer it. The sight of a policeman and policewoman unsettles me. 'Is everything okay?' I ask.

'Are you Mr. Alastair Richmond?' the policewoman asks.

'That's me.'

'May we speak with you inside?'

'Sure.' I bring them through to the lounge and Rachael startles when she sees them.

They take a seat, and after they introduce themselves, the policewoman asks, 'Do you know a Mr. and Mrs. Baylor, Mr. Richmond?'

'Yes,' I say, trying to conceal my nerves. Rachael reaches for my hand and holds it tenderly.

'We have bad news, Mr. Richmond. Their bodies were found at 9:30 a.m. last Sunday. Their deaths are not being treated as suspicious.' The news of Mr. Baylor's death comes as a genuine shock. 'It is thought that Mr. Baylor poisoned his wife with cyanide and then drank the poison himself after calling us.'

'That's terrible,' Rachael and I echo.

'There is something else that we need to tell you. This concerns you directly, Mr. Richmond...'

THE HOST OF
HAWKETH HOUSE

A gatha welcomes me; we are firm friends now. I glance at *The Dream* to see the new, young faces painted in.

'Won't you dance with me?' Agatha asks.

'Of course, my dear,' I say.

I lead her to the doorway of the ballroom.

Christophe has been expecting us. 'Ladies and gentlemen,' he announces to the crowd. 'It's time for the first dance. Tonight, we swing to an old favourite: Ruth Etting. Now, let me introduce, The Hostess of The Dream and The Host of The House.'

The crowd cheers, and Christophe hits the gramophone's arm. Agatha and I dance to one of my favourite songs: *Ten cents a dance...*

We dance slowly, our moves well-practised. 'Agatha, my dear,' I say, 'we have a guest coming to stay tomorrow.'

'Who is it?'

'A Frenchmen by the name of Monsieur Jacques Glapion. Two nights. He runs an appreciation society for the author Edgar Allan Poe. He is also a key member of the underground jazz scene in Paris.'

'Children? A wife?'

'A wife, but I suspect he is trapped in the relationship.'

'Why do you say that?'

'Something he wrote about wanting time on his own. And judging by his posts on modern media, I suspect he may be gay.'

'That is not a problem, we welcome all kinds, but be sure to press him hard to discover whether his wife or any of his secret friends know about his visit here. Before dinner, make sure you have all of the letters that you sent. Do not ask me for a verdict, if not. If I am not thoroughly satisfied, I will not allow him to enter.'

'Of course.'

'Excellent, I am excited at the prospect of having a Frenchman in The Dream. It will please Christophe to use his second language.'

'I'm sure.'

'I must say that I am thoroughly pleased with you as The Host of The House. Your teaching of Morse code is exceptional, your renovation of the shared bedroom downstairs is remarkable, and your wife is doing a sterling job of making sure our new guests are happy here.'

'Thank you.'

The next song comes on and everyone joins us. Christophe takes a young Mrs. Baylor's hand. My wife dances with a handsome Mr. Baylor. I overhear their conversation. Mr. Baylor is asking how our trip to Japan was.

'Oh, Japan was wonderful,' my wife says. 'The temples were beautiful, and the food was delicious. Do you not miss food, Delbert?'

'I don't. I'm never hungry and taste is a forgotten memory.'

'We have just booked flights to New Orleans,' my wife adds. 'I must ask Christophe about all the things that we should see and experience there.'

'Are you staying at the house?' Mr. Baylor asks.

'We are indeed. We are really excit—'

Trumpets blare, cutting off their conversation. A crowd favourite, "Button Up Your Overcoat", plays.

The rhythm breaks to something much livelier. My feet race Agatha's. I catch sight of my wife switching to dance with Christophe as Mr. Baylor sweeps his wife off her feet. I beam as I cast a glance their way because Mrs. Baylor's forgiveness has not come easily for him. I shift my focus back to the high-tempo dance with Agatha. Our moves are well-practised, then she smirks at the song's mention of "bootleg hooch". This is the cue for us to commence the finale of our routine.

Agatha twirls into me, wrapping herself in my arms. I catch her, then spin her back and release her out into the centre of the ballroom. She pirouettes through the glittery mass of revellers as an instrumental bursts into life. I erupt into a fit of "air" trumpeting. Many of the men also join me, and we all perform with exaggerated vigour. It becomes a frantic affair, full of colour and joy. Then, as the song fades out to a mellower tune, I approach the Baylors.

'May I steal your wife for this dance, Delbert?' I ask, offering out my hand.

'By all means,' he says.

The youthful Mrs. Baylor gives me a kind smile as she accepts my invitation. Her frostiness towards me is a distant memory. She is now unburdened and purrs in my arms as we swing and sway.

———◦———

I wake beside my beautiful wife. 'Darling, did you speak to Christophe?' I ask.

'Yes, I have enough suggestions to fill our whole week in New Orleans.'

'Fantastic.'

I get up and inspect the grey hairs in the mirror. I smile. Most people fear turning grey. It signals the beginning of the end, but in this house, it is just the end of the beginning. I did not expect Mr. Baylor to bequeath this house and its fortune to me, but every day since has been filled with immense joy and love and fulfilment.

Later that morning, I blow out the candles in all the rooms and make breakfast, then I climb Hawne Pike, one of the hills overlooking the house.

My wife spends the rest of the morning painting. She has really taken to her new hobby. Shortly after noon, she leaves for Skelgate station, and I prepare for our guest.

———◦———

I hear Rachael creak open the door when she returns. That is my cue to descend the stairs. I am wearing my tuxedo; I find first impressions are so important, and looking down on someone establishes authority. I stand at the point where the marble staircase turns.

The man looks nervous. 'Bonjour, Mr. Richmond,' he says.

'Monsieur Glapion, I presume,' I say. 'Follow me, please.'

I walk up the stairs. The house creaks to tell me that he is following. I lead him past all the possessions on display, to which I have added my own.

'Zis 'ouse is very beautiful, Mr. Richmond,' our guest says. 'You must enjoy living 'ere.'

'Monsieur Glapion, I have arranged for you to have the room with the view over Lake Linketh.'

'Zat is most excellent. Thank you.'

I walk slowly and sedately so that I do not disturb the dreamers. And at no point do I look behind because I do not want Monsieur Glapion to see just how broadly I am grinning. After all, why wouldn't I be pleased? I am The Host of Hawketh House.

GHOST STORIES FOR CHRISTMAS

Winter

THE RAVENS' SPELL

Winter, a long time ago

In a world without laughter, a strange noise wakes the people of an ancient town. The residents are accustomed to the oppressive cackling of ravens, but tonight, all is eerily quiet—except for the solitary call which stirs something strange within the people's hearts.

The townsfolk, wearing thin rags, grumble as they emerge from cold homes to silence the call. Barefoot, they tread on frosty cobbles and walk beneath icicle archways. The residents do not work together, and consequently, they are poor.

Dim streetlights cast narrow alleys in a glow devoid of colour. Tall, stone houses funnel the townsfolk towards the square. The ravens sit still, no longer cavorting atop the antiquated rooftops and steeples.

The strange chuckle multiplies, more residents wake, and miserable faces begin to crack. Another new noise is heard—a jingle.

Streets branch off the town square like tentacles, and from each, people converge. At the centre is a man with a bushy, white beard and a bright, red suit. He wraps each resident in thick clothes, hands them slippers and a small bell, and embraces them with a warm hug. He spreads his joy and soon the whole town is awake and in merry song.

There is music, colour and mouths that curl curiously at both ends. The ravens flee; their gloomy spell is broken. The jolly man leaves on a peculiar chariot, but he is not forgotten.

In time, the clothes perish and the slippers crumble, but they work together to make new ones. The true gift was kindness. Every year, the new community celebrate with a great festival because now they know happiness and cheer and laughter.

THE GIFT OF A NAME

25th December, 1879

E ach night, I wander from graveyard to graveyard. Those I meet know only their names. Me? I don't even know that!

This existence of mine, so bleak and dreary. No sleep, no memory, no rest. But if I can find my name etched in cold stone, I may finally gain salvation.

A full moon reawakens my senses, but it's foolish to say I feel human when *they* walk through me like I'm nothing. And with no presence or name, how am I not nothing?

This snowy churchyard twinkles in the glow from candles, placed in decorated trees, that flicker in a light breeze. Dressed warmly and huddled together, the humans join us, and they're in merry cheer. Their breath freezes as they sing of a silent night, yet this is anything but.

Curious, I follow their parade through this quiet village. Their feet crunch fresh snow and smiling families emerge from homes laden with colourful wreaths to greet them. It stirs something in me. Emotion, yes, but also something else—a memory.

The further I follow them, the more this déjà vu grows. I've wandered, aimless and lost, for so long, but I've been here before—I can feel it! And this strange festival... was I once a part of it?

'Merry Christmas,' are the calls between neighbours across the street. Yes, I know this. I peer through a window and find a young boy sitting beside a fire, his eyes fixated upon brightly wrapped presents under a decorative tree.

A memory hits me, of me as the child. I recall a friendly, booming voice, 'Merry Christmas, Edgar Shaw.' That old man who handed me a gift, has given me another tonight—my name.

I rush back to the cemetery, shouting as rapturously as the villagers. Now I search for this key to peace and joy amongst the snow-capped tombstones. My search goes on and on, but then I stop.

Beneath a candlelit yew tree is my promised gift. Seeing my name is like retrieving a lost thread of my humanity. And there is not just one name. There are many Shaws. This is my place of rest—*our* place of rest. But what is this—this sweet noise that I hear? My family—they're calling my name.

MY CORPSE CANDLE

Spring

MY CORPSE CANDLE

April 30th, 2026

The cliffs near Conby mirror the jagged shoreline below, as powerful gusts drive sea spray up and over the clifftops in rolling waves of wind. Beyond the cliff edge, a lingering cloud of sea spray sparkles under bright moonlight, and it washes inland with each rushing gust. It drifts across a grassy plain, weaves through the tombstones of an ancient cemetery, crosses a coastal road, and climbs the slopes of distant farmland.

Amongst the swirling, glimmering mist from the salty sea shines a steady blue-green light impervious to the wind and the water. This solitary candle is not borne of flame, and just as the spectral glow of the moon remains untouched by earthly elements, so too is this. Its sharp, concentrated light appears like a shard of moonlight, and it hovers tantalisingly close to the cliff edge.

Perching on the cemetery's belfry, a raven cries a warning in the direction of the ghost light. Its croaks draw the attention of a farmer walking along a rural lane overlooking the cliffs. For someone in his early twenties, the man harbours coarse stubble. He takes a few paces before pausing beside a cherry tree. Colour drains from his complexion as fast as gusts rip petals of fresh blossom from the tree. The petals shrivel as they land in muddy puddles—a pitiful demise portending his own. The man's countenance freezes in a terrified rictus. It is a pleasure to witness.

The young farmer, Danny Wilcox, rubs his eyes in the vain hope that the light might disappear. He glances left, then right—then back again, unable to tear his gaze away for too long. 'Please God, tell me it's not... Tell me it's not my Corpse Candle.' Danny takes a few tentative steps backwards then sprints back the way he came.

The town's first lamppost stands outside a large stone building, with an illuminated sign reading: "The Inn at The Edge". Danny bursts through the door into the inn's dim-lit warmth.

Only a few small groups occupy the pub due to the late hour. A barmaid cleans at the bar, and a bearded older man heads for the exit.

'Are you leaving already?' Danny says to the older man.

'It's quiet tonight, and Sandra doesn't seem interested in my ramblings,' the man replies.

'Tony, I need to talk to someone. Can you stay a little longer? I'll get a round in.'

'All right,' Tony says, bemused. 'Don't have to ask me twice.' Questions hover about his lips, but he hesitates to voice them until they are lubricated by the promised free drink.

A flicker of suspicion cuts across Tony's crinkled face as he struggles to understand how he's managed to score a free drink without first pretending he's owed one. Usually, any drink that came his way carried an undertone of mockery or was a pitying donation to silence his thinly veiled pleas.

Danny carries two pints to a quiet corner, and as Tony follows, he gazes about as if venturing into new territory. Despite his regular appearance at the inn, this spot lies far from patrons to pester and away from his usual seat at the bar. For Tony, this is out of his comfort zone. Sitting opposite Danny in the gloom of an old lamp, Tony savours his first sip as if it were the start of some new adventure.

'Can you keep a secret?' Danny asks. His expression is one of a man who knows the question is futile.

'My secrecy can be bought easily,' Tony says, raising his glass.

'I'll put twenty quid behind the bar for you.'

'That'll do it!'

Danny sneers, knowing full well that this man would likely blackmail him for beers forevermore, but that price would be worth paying if he got to see even a slice of that *forevermore*.

'Do you remember a boy named George Falstaff?' Danny asks.

'Oh, the boy who jumped off the cliffs and died? Years ago now. People don't talk about him much any-more.'

'What if I told you that it was an accident, not sui-cide?' Danny says.

He's going to pretend it was an accident, is he? He deserves what's coming.

'Oh, this is interesting... What did you do?' Tony asks with a smirk, knowing that such a secret could be a veritable treasure chest of amber ale.

'That summer,' Danny starts, and Tony leans in, 'five of us were bored and drinking by the cliffs. We saw George searching for crabs in the rockpools below. He was always a bit of a hermit, so we joked that he was searching for his own kind. A cruel joke, but, in our boredom, we invited him up to join us. Offered him a beer.' Lie. 'Being a loner, we thought he'd probably never kissed a girl or drank alcohol. We thought it'd be funny to see his reaction to both.'

'My girlfriend, Sophie, invited him up. He was eager to join us.' Lie. 'We knew him from school, and I remember being surprised that this nerd was somehow good at basketball. I thought he could be an alright lad.'

'He accepted a beer, and we got chatting. We were teasing him a bit, but that's all it was. Sophie was a little cruel by teasing him in a different way, touching him, making him think she liked him. She was his first kiss, and such was his attachment that he defended her when I implied something rude.

'We were sat on the grassy plain by the old cemetery. Our friend, Chris picked up a handful of stones by the cliff edge and started throwing them off. Conby Bay was around the headland to the right, no one came here, except lonely hermit-boy George. There was no danger in throwing the stones, and it became a bit of competition to see who could throw one to reach the sea.

'That's when George got overly competitive, trying to show off to Soph.' Lie. 'On one of his throws, he got too close to the edge and slipped. He seemed to catch his fall, but a rock came loose and gave way. Before we could process what had just happened, we heard a thump from the rockpools below. Like the scared teenagers we were, we ran. I never liked the fact that people thought this little lonely hermit-boy committed suicide, but us saying it was an accident wouldn't have changed anything. That's the truth of it.'

Outrageous!

Tony finishes a sip, already halfway through his beer, and says, 'OK... There's something that doesn't add up.'

'Oh really? What's that then?' Danny says, taking an aggressive form of defence.

'You left here in good spirits earlier. Then you rushed back in twenty minutes later, pale, and determined to tell someone—anyone—this tale. What happened outside?'

'You're right, but I have more to tell,' Danny says. 'Do you know what happened to the others I was with that day? Dwight, Chris, Rhys, and my old flame, Sophie.'

'No. Go on...'

'They're all dead!'

'What? Are you serious?'

'Yeah.'

'I'm sorry to hear that,' Tony says solemnly. 'You know… I'm in here every night, talking to all the locals, getting all the goss. How is it I don't know about the deaths of four locals who were part of the dead boy's… *accident*…'

'It *was* an accident!' Danny snaps.

Lie.

'Sounds like someone saw you…'

'It's way weirder than that…' Danny starts. 'Dwight was the first, about a year afterwards. The others moved away at some point or other—that's probably why you've not heard.'

'Dwight's family moved to a house by the sea in Skelgate, then one rainy night, he never returned home after visiting a friend. You'll know how notorious those choppy waters are. Someone reported a young man swimming out to the Isles of Yystrya, and a few days later his body was discovered washed up on those rocky islands. But that wasn't the only strange occurrence that night. There were no reports of any sounds like the siren calls those islands are known for, but there were several reports of an alluring blue-green light glowing by the rainy shoreline. One person reported it on land, another reported it moving out towards the islands. Do you know what it might have been?' Tony shook his head. 'Have you ever heard of the legend of the Corpse Candle?'

'No,' Tony says.

'It is said that the Corpse Candle is a ghostly blue-green light, and a sighting of it will always be followed by someone's death at or near its location. It's an omen of death. These reports of an ethereal light burning brightly on a rainy night were followed by the death of my friend Dwight.'

'Do you believe it?' Tony asks.

'I didn't at the time. I learnt more about the myth, including similar reports across Britain and Ireland. Many relate it to Stingy Jack of the Lantern in Ireland. I took all these myths as a flight of fancy. That was until the death of my girlfriend, Sophie, the following spring.

'One night, whilst she was staying with her grand-parents in Elderigg, she called me in amazement. She said there was a pixie dancing at the end of the garden, and she was going to meet it. She described how it had an alluring turquoise glow, but when she got close, it fled through a hedgerow and climbed the valley.

'It was a warm night, and wearing just her nightie, she followed it. She was walking barefoot and talking to me on the phone. I could hear her saying, "Don't be scared little one. I just want to say hello." She was talking to it as if it were a cat. I became irate and de-manded that she go back to her grandparents. She just ignored me, saying, "It's enchanting" or "It wants me to follow" or "It's taking me somewhere magical." I was mad. I shouted at her, and her phone cut off. Later they found her phone on the ground not far from the village—she'd just discarded it. Truly, I believe she was in a trance.'

'That doesn't sound like a stalker. What happened to her?' Tony asks.

'Her body was found at the base of Castle Draymere.'

'Castle Draymere!'

'I know! It's about an hour's hike from her grand-parents' house. The ethereal light caught her in such a spell that she walked over an hour, in just her night-clothes, across muddy hills and then scaled those castle ruins. You can climb to the battlements at the top of Castle Draymere, and she must have followed all the way along to where the walls collapse. She fell and broke her neck.'

'I'm so sorry,' Tony says, consoling Danny, who purses his lips, holding back his emotion.

'Ever since that day,' Danny says, 'I've believed the myth of the corpse candle. It could only take some un-earthly phenomenon to make my bone-idol girlfriend walk such a distance like that. But... I didn't think about it targeting the five of us until I learnt of Chris' death the following spring.'

'Spring?' Tony asks.

'You're noticing a pattern too… And not just spring—always around the end of April, start of May.'

'Was that when George died?'

'That's the weird thing, no. He died in August. Have you ever heard of something called Witches' Night?'

'No.'

'Walpurgisnacht?'

'No, but I don't much like the sound of it.'

'All these old myths and legends refer to the changing of the seasons. There's supposedly two nights notorious for strange phenomena like this. Halloween, of course, but also the last night in April. Some call it these names. I've heard Beltane too. It's all mad pagan shit. And the more I think about it, the more I think the light first appears on that exact night.'

'So, each of your friends saw this corpse candle, followed it, and ended up dead?'

'Yeah.'

'What if they simply didn't follow it?'

'Chris didn't initially,' Danny says. 'He called me from his top floor flat in Kirkene saying he was looking at this strange light towards Wisburn Bog. He took a photo and sent it to me. It was hard to make out, but there was something. He didn't go the first night. So, even though he skipped the last night in April, it was still there the next night. He called me again, you see, said he'd checked it out. Chris was a rational man; he felt stupid being scared the night before and, during the day, he'd learnt that bogs release gases. And this was cited as the explanation behind the will-o'-the-wisp and the original jack-o'-lantern.

'Buoyed by reason, Chris dared himself to go investigate. He called me on his way out of Kirkene, commenting how people in horror movies never make phone calls or use technology to their aid. He felt protected talking to me, but I reminded him that Soph had done the same thing. He ignored my passionate pleas for him to return too.

'Chris walked the country lane and said after a while, "It must be moving away from me. How else could I have seen it from my bedroom window, yet I can't see any lights from the town now?" Soon he added, "At last! I'm getting closer. It's at the edge of the bog."

'We were talking all the while. He was in a lively mood; it was an adventure to him. He sounded so like Soph, mesmerised by this thing. He didn't call it a pixie or anything, but I could hear in his voice that he was enchanted by it. "I'm nearly there," he said full of excitement. "It's a little into the bog, but it's not too muddy." A little later, he added, "It's drifting away like a balloon in a light breeze, but I'm gaining! It's starting to get boggy now though."

'"Whoa! My foot just sunk right in. It's soaked!" Chris said. He was laughing. "Oh God! It's gone in really deep." The laughter in Chris' voice shifted to louder, harsher gasps like the sound of someone catching their breath after too long underwater. "Shit! Danny, my other foot's gone in too." Fear cut Chris' voice, and it was so sharp that it barbed my heart. "Danny mate... I think I'm stuck. Shit! I'm in trouble here. Every time I move, I sink deeper. The candle's circling me now. Danny..." There was a quiver in his voice. Then he cried, "Danny!"

'The line went dead. I knew where he was, so I called the emergency services. Nothing. Wisburn Bog retains his corpse to this day.

'It left just me and Rhys, but Rhys panicked. Neither of us could deny it any longer; something was hunting down the five of us. Rhys didn't wait for it to come for him. He moved to Wales and never told anyone from Deaconshire, not even me, where he went. He judged that someone—some friend or family member of George—was getting their revenge.'

'Did it catch up with him?' Tony asks.

'Rhys had gone completely off the grid, and when spring next rolled around, I wondered why I hadn't done the same. I had been obnoxiously in denial. I went from dismissing the idea to believing I would be next. As I hadn't moved, I was the easier target. I isolated myself at home for a few days, thinking if I didn't look out the window, the ghost flame couldn't lure me out. Then I got a text from an unknown number. It simply read: "It's found me."

'It was another week before I heard that Rhys had died, in a barn fire supposedly. No idea how that happened. Now I know fleeing is futile. I've been expecting the Grim Reaper, but it's mad to believe in the supernatural. Every day when the world remains corporeal and sane, you just wonder, maybe—just maybe—it's not real. It won't catch up to me.'

Ignorance suits you well.

'Why have you decided to tell someone tonight then?' Tony asks.

'Because I've just fucking seen it!' Danny says.

'What? Tonight?'

'What day is it?' Danny asks.

'Oh...'

'Yeah... My corpse candle, it's out there now, waiting for me by the cliffs.' Danny points to the door. 'Go out and take a look.'

'Are you kidding me? I'm not going anywhere near that,' Tony says.

Danny grumbles. 'The common thing about each incident is that, despite me being on the phone, each of my friends has investigated it alone. No one has witnessed it and reported back what actually happens when you get close to the corpse candle. If I go alone and die, then that information will die along with me.

This legend pre-dates me and my friends, so what's to say this won't happen again? If someone came as a witness, they may learn what it truly is and how to extinguish it. That person could save a life, perhaps even tonight!' Danny shoots Tony a knowing glance. 'If someone did that, the bar here would be permanently free.'

Tony stares gloomily upon the little beer in his glass. His hand trembles as he takes another sip then looks up at Danny, and says, 'I know my life ain't worth shit, and I don't have any smarts. But I know when a man's telling the truth. I believe your omen, and I'm so sorry for you. I will do what you need me to do—get your affairs in order or pass on a message. But I ain't stupid enough to go chasing death omens or fairy lights. And neither should you.'

'I don't want to go chasing it neither,' Danny says. 'But the omen has appeared four times, and each time someone has met a supposedly accidental death. Maybe I never leave my home, but what's to say a fire doesn't start whilst I'm asleep? How can I escape it?'

'I don't know.' Tony finishes his drink and gazes forlornly at the empty glass. He glances at Danny and then down at the table, almost scared to look at the doomed man. 'I'm sorry to do this, but if the omen comes true, I don't want no part in it. Sandra, behind the bar, has seen me chatting to you. If anything happens, suspicion will fall my way. I can't help you in this fight.'

'Don't be a coward!' Danny snaps.

'I'm sorry.'

'Your life is worth shit! What a waste spending every night here. The barmaids don't even want to talk to you. Grow a pair and come fight this thing.'

Tony stands up, but Danny grabs his arm. 'Are you just going to let me die?' Tony wrestles to get away but Danny holds firm. 'Stop being the pathetic local drunk and do something with your life. You're a coward.'

'You're right,' Tony says. 'I am a coward, and I drink away my problems. I can't help you fight mystical foes, but I can make something of my life. This is my last ever beer.' Danny's laugh is full of sarcasm. 'I mean it this time.'

'You're a lying coward. No better than vermin. Go and scurry away.' Danny releases Tony's arm. As Tony sheepishly walks out, Danny shouts another insult his way.

When the door closes behind Tony, Danny thumps the table. 'That fucking coward,' Danny shouts. 'Why couldn't he have taken my place?' Danny gazes around for someone to rage at, only to discover he's the last remaining patron. His expression changes as fear pushes through his anger. And then, as Sandra returns and calls time, he drops his head to the table.

Sandra goes to the back, leaving Danny alone. He snivels to himself. Good. Danny whimpers, 'Why did we do it? Why does it have to come now?'

Sandra calls time again.

'Fuck it! Fine. I'm going... never to come back.' Danny storms out.

———◦———

Moonlight and a bitter chill greet Danny who pauses. He looks to the rural lane home and then to the coastal road. Trees obscure the cliffside and the cemetery, but Danny knows what's waiting there. He looks between the two. With a huff, he says to himself, 'I'm no fucking coward.'

Danny marches off along the coast road, leaving the pub, the lamplights, and the town behind. No cars pass on the road. Trees blow, and the raven still croaks its alarm call. The cliffside cemetery comes into view. Sea spray, sparkling in the lunar light, swirls amongst the hoary headstones like ghosts dancing an ethereal waltz. And then, a glow as mystical as the aurora reappears hovering in the same spot above the grassy plain beside the cliff edge.

Does this bastard really think he can come out on top? For him to lie about past events shows he has no genuine remorse. He deserves what's coming.

Danny peels off the road and onto the grassy plain. Sea spray continues to billow up and over the edge like tides of moonlight. The corpse candle flickers above a spot close to the edge but also far enough from it that you wouldn't fall to the rocks below if you slipped.

Danny slows his approach, narrowing his eyes and peering around. He clenches his fist, in anticipation of something that has not yet manifested. The corpse candle's lustre shimmers through colours of blue and green, with flashes of purple and yellow and flickers of some colours that are as intangible as they are magical. This spectral flame holds Danny's gaze, his brow furrowed in fear, his jaw agape in wonder.

Danny pauses before the flame, squatting down to meet it at eye level. He puts one hand on the grass, keeping firm his contact with the ground. The edge is metres away, no gust of wind could take him over.

Danny knows the location; the ghost flame burns where his evil deed was borne. Danny reaches out with his other hand and holds it to the flame as if to warm his hand, but he looks between the flame and his hand—there is no heat. Danny pushes his hand further, soon to contact the flame. He glances around once more, then jolts his hand into the flame and quickly returns it. Nothing.

Danny looks to his hand then he touches the flame once more. Danny's hand passes through, there is no burning. He then wafts his hand through the flame, but it has no effect. The flame does not react to his touch. Danny then spits and blows at the flame. Nothing. He pauses, not knowing what to do. He came to fight and confront, yet nothing has happened.

This is Danny's first experience of what life as a ghost will be like. To not be able to touch, to not be seen, to not have any effect—it's painful. But Danny is no ghost—the worlds of the corporeal and the ethereal interact very rarely. But there are nights—as Danny has realised—when the veil between the two worlds is at its thinnest. As winter transitions to summer—a night when April transitions to May—is one such night. And tonight's near-full moon adds further spectral energy to enhance such effects.

Danny, perceiving nothing, stands once more. He walks through the flame, looks around and takes a few steps towards the cliff edge. He gets as close as he dares, and then his shoulders drop as his fear and apprehension fade.

This is the moment I've waited almost five years for. I lit my corpse candle earlier this evening and have since followed the man who threw me off this cliff. I tailed him as he went to the inn and attempted to confess to Tony. I had hoped to see remorse, but all I saw was *lies*. Lies upon lies. A long life was not to be for me, and I'll make it so for Danny too.

I step into my corpse candle as Danny turns away from the cliff, his guard down. The ghost flame explodes; its spectral power courses through me. Danny staggers backwards in surprise. He shields his eyes from the light but then he takes a harder look. 'George?' he says.

The candle is no more; instead, its lustre illuminates my ghostly being. I stand before my murderer, the ghost that he made. My new power is ephemeral; I do not have long to make my mark. I step towards Danny, and he steps back.

Danny was the ringleader of his friends. He saw a boy playing in the rockpools, but their shouts were insults, not invites. Rhys and Chris hurled rocks at me, then on Danny's instruction, they came down to the shore and dragged me up to this cliff edge. Sophie taunted me, saying how I'd never know a woman's touch. And Danny forced me to look over the edge. He questioned how I would fall. Would my brains spill out or would my legs snap? He pointed out the cemetery, said he'd watch as they lowered what remained of me in. He teased how no one would witness it and how he had a cover story. His act was premeditated.

After my life was cut short, I had a choice. Accept a heavenly embrace and rest in my grave or wander like Jack of the Lantern with only a small ember to illuminate the darkness. This ember is a piece of one's own soul, and once a spirit rests, their soul can no longer fragment. Five years for a spirit without rest is a torment tantamount to five years for a mortal without sleep. But on these spectral nights, the shard of my soul enflames to become a visible lure for me to enact my retribution. And with the power of the moon near-full, my whole being straddles both ethereal and corporeal realms.

I take another step forwards. Danny steps back and slips. He regains his balance but glances behind. He's at the edge. He cannot back away from me anymore. I purposely cast my flame a little from the edge, so I could have this moment to face him down.

I take another step towards my murderer. 'Please,' Danny begs. 'I'm sorry, George. I truly am.' Another lie. He doesn't realise that I've been a spectre at his shoulder tonight, witnessing his lies. I step forwards again.

My corpse candle will fade soon, but whilst Danny can see me, I can touch him... And I can push him. Danny begs and grovels, yet he seems ashamed to look at me.

The moonlit mist behind Danny shimmers like a heavenly cloud—a place I once deserved to be. Yet Danny and his friends always belonged below. Far far below.

My corpse candle has lured the others to a choppy ocean, castle ruins, a bog, and a tinderbox. But now that we've returned to where it all began, I will do the deed with my own hands. Danny's eyes lock onto mine. He can see their resolve. 'Don't!' he cries. I take another step forwards, so we stand face to face.

A ghost harbours an existence without touch, smell, or taste, yet my corpse candle reignites such senses. I reach out and touch Danny's chest. His heart pounds against my hands, a countdown entering single digits. His foul breath stings my nostrils, and the salty ocean tantalises my tongue. I relish the return of all five senses, but most of all, I savour the sight of the whites of my murderer's eyes as he stands frozen in fear.

Without a word, I push. Danny's eyes flare as he falls away. His limbs flail, and he cries out. The glimmering mist swallows him. I wait expectantly... I wonder if his brains will spill out or if his legs will snap. Given the mist, I will probably never know. A crack cuts through the night. I turn away from the cliff edge as the lustre of my corpse candle begins to fade. Once gone, I and it will never be seen again. I walk towards the cemetery; my thoughts can turn to resting now.

A man runs out from the gloom of the graveyard. Tony has been watching from the cemetery. If he was the coward that Danny made out, he wouldn't be here and approaching me now. 'Please,' Tony says, 'leave this town alone now that you've had your vengeance.'

While my words may still carry to his ears, I reply, 'Honour your promise of sobriety, and I vow not to return.'

Tony's face turns pale as he realises that I observed his promise in the pub. And if I could witness that, what else might I witness? He would have no way to know if I was watching him or not.

'Yes, George. I promise,' he says. And with that, Tony hurries back to the town. I never intend to light a corpse candle again, but Tony doesn't know that. Seeing the man's reaction, I am confident that he will heed his vow.

My effect on Tony may be inadvertent, but nonetheless, it is an effect. I am a ghost, yet nearly five years after my death, I can still make a lasting impact on the living world. I will take my rest now, but it is some comfort that my final act upon the corporeal realm is to improve a life as opposed to selfish revenge. The five-year wait may be worth it for that alone.

The cemetery's bell rings out with deep, earth-shattering peals. It is the Eldritch Chime; mortal ears will not hear it, yet a startled raven flies away. These tolls mark the passing of someone from the corporeal to the ethereal realm—a chime of death. It signals the completion of my unfinished business. I shall be a restless spirit no more.

Approaching the cemetery gates, my corpse candle burns out. My light on this world is no more. I pass through the closed lychgate; my touch will no longer be felt here. I wander through the graveyard to a stone tablet that catches the lunar light. Etched into the stone, it records the name: George Falstaff. No wreaths or memorials are to be found here, but cherry blossom dusts the ground before my headstone. At least Nature remembers me fondly.

I take one last look around me, my gaze lingering on all I leave behind. I let out a heavy and wistful sigh. It is time. With a final step, I descend into my grave. At long last, I can rest in peace.

A PAINTING BY MAGDALENA ROSE

Summer

A PAINTING BY
MAGDALENA ROSE (I)

August, 1909

C hina chattered as Mr. and Mrs. Hayes sipped tea
on their balcony. Mrs. Hayes happily watched
a summer sun setting behind distant hills, whilst Mr.
Hayes' eyes were upon his wife, whose wavy, blonde
hair seemed to glow with the day's golden hour. Mrs.
Hayes' looked down to an emporium on the street below. A variety of curios was on display of the blackened
building and a sign wrought in copper-metal read,
"Hayes Antique Shoppe".

'Do you remember how close we came to selling the
copper, my darling?' Mrs. Hayes said to her husband,

a young, smartly dressed man with a trimmed moustache and mutton chops.

'Most certainly, my dear Doris.' Mr. Hayes replied.

'For the first time, I feel unburdened by financial worry. You've been very shrewd, Richard. I admit I didn't share your conviction.'

'That's kind of you to concede. I was sure a valuable sign would attract those with money. No street urchins like those your father had to put up with in this town.'

'Quite. I daresay we owe a good deal of our change in fortunes to the painting by that vulgar artist. You sold it again today, you say?'

'Leased it again, yes, my dear, to a dandy of a chap—Mr. Henry Glover.'

'How long till its return, do you suppose?'

'Usually it is a few weeks. Last time was merely a few days. I'm hopeful that it might be up for sale by the end of next week.'

'That is remarkable. Truly. I'm surprised you haven't sought another of these horrid paintings. That one alone is a firm pillar of your business,' Mrs. Hayes said.

Mr. Hayes laughed. 'You hated that painting, now you imply that I should purchase another?'

'I care not what you do in your emporium so long as our finances are secure and our home is free of that ghastly artwork.'

'But you are mistaken, my dear; that painting is a fine piece. The lady is beautiful, the church majestic, and the way the grassy hills glisten under the moonlight is marvellous, indeed.'

'So, the scene is pleasant, but it was created by that dreadful painter. What's her name again?'

'Magdalena Rose, my dear.'

'Magdalena? What heathen corner of the continent did she come here from?'

'She is supposedly a daughter of Deaconshire,' Mr. Hayes said.

'No one like that could be born here. She is the Mary Shelley of artists. How I abhor all that she is. She made such vile paintings; one of them traumatised my dear Papa. Such devilry on canvas, all for what, a shock? Was being a woman not enough of a shock? She has single-handedly undermined the Suffragette's valiant cause. She is no woman but a devil.'

'Those paintings got her notoriety, but no one could stomach to even glimpse them let alone hang one in their homes. And yet, without her former work, her newer paintings would not be so valuable.'

'How can anyone even consider hanging that dev-il-woman's artwork in their home or business?'

'Her "Rose Petal" oil paintings capture salvation in art form,' Mr. Hayes said. 'She was a frenzied, wicked woman capable of conjuring unspeakable horrors from her mind and graphically depicting them on canvas. No one wanted anything to do with such devilry and she was outcast. Her return came secretly, selling to private sellers under a different name and never once making an appearance. When it was revealed that Magdalena Rose was indeed the artist of the Rose Petals, well... Today's buyer put it like this: "It is as though her old paintings have been exorcised. The devil is gone, and what this Rose Petal shows is the power and the glory of God.'"

'Folly!' Mrs. Hayes said.

'There had been rumours that she'd found God, and what other possible cause could there be for such a drastic change in art style?'

'That woman is devious; she cannot be trusted. By using a pseudonym, it is evident that she tricked good people.'

'Perhaps "Magdalena" was the pseudonym, my dear?'

Mrs. Hayes shrugged then turned to face a red sky, the sun having now set. A new thought came to her, 'Is it not suspicious to you that her painting returns so readily?'

Mr. Hayes glanced at his wife and dried a sweaty palm on his suit trousers. 'Once my customers have dazzled their esteemed guests with such works of art, they have little use for them. Not unlike how the copper of my signage elevates my status to those who have only time for snap judgements.'

'So, they return them willingly after their event is past?' Mrs. Hayes returned her gaze to her husband. She narrowed her eyes.

'Yes, my dear. You doubted my signage and my purchases, and here we are quaffing the best tea in our new apartment, a veritable penthouse compared to our prior lodgings.'

'My feelings are quite mixed. I shall leave you to sort the business, but dealings in works of a devil will only poison you.'

'A devil come angel, my dear.'

'Pah! Save your sales pitch for your clients. The fruit may seem juicy, but I believe it is rotten at the core.'

A moment of silence lay between them. Mr. Hayes wiped his sweaty palm on his trousers once more and regarded his wife's expression. It was evident to him that her mind was racing with questions. 'You should not worry about—'

Mrs. Hayes cut him off, asking, 'And how is it that you decided to lease her painting?'

'Quite by accident, my dear. But please do not worry about my work. Have I not made you happy?'

'Very much so.'

'Then please, let us enjoy this fine summer's evening,' Mr. Hayes said pouring two more cups of tea from a teapot.

Mrs. Hayes smiled once more, lifting the cloud that the mere mention of Magdalena Rose had brought. 'We have so much to look forward to now,' she said, turning her gaze back to the red sky. A look of serenity washed over her once more.

Mr. Hayes smiled too, but it belied something different. It was a smile of ambition, a smile of success, a smile of a man who knew more than he let on.

A PAINTING BY
MAGDALENA ROSE (II)

The monotonous rattle of the carriage and the rhythmic clop of horse's hooves continued as the golden hour turned blue. The journey from Lyeminster to Lordale was not a short one, and Mr. Henry Glover had asked the coachman to take his time on the rutted lanes. He had a precious painting to transport. Henry had also opted for a four-wheeled coach for the extra space and comfort, as compared with a hansom cab. The young brown-haired man was alone in the cabin, and his purchase was on the cushioned seat opposite.

Mr. Hayes had been attentive in wrapping the art-work to protect it in transit, yet only a few minutes into the journey, Henry had unfurled much of it to gaze upon the oil painting as he travelled. The setting sun had shone in from behind the carriage illuminating the artwork with its tender touch, and now it shimmered in the soft light of the coach's oil lanterns. Perhaps it was a little negligent to expose the painting to sunlight, he thought, but this was only a lease. Of course, such a fine piece deserved protecting, but was it not the primary purpose of art to be savoured? That it had instigated an unusual impatience in him demonstrated its magic.

Savour the painting, he surely did. He looked upon the woman in the painting as if she were his very own darling. As a bachelor of modest wealth, dreams of beauty were not wholly unwarranted. The entire scene depicted what he was striving so hard for: an attractive young woman with fire in both her hair and her eyes; an ornate gothic church where faith could flourish; and rolling hills in the background where one could enjoy the peace and serenity of nature. And didn't the cool tones of the lunar lighting just reinforce a timeless quality? It made him wish for tranquillity and gave him hope that such a moment may last for eternity.

The title of the painting was simple but curious, "Rose Petal VI". Henry knew of the Rose Petals, but this was the first he'd seen. It implied there were at least six, but how many there were in total was a mystery. Did "Rose" refer to the reddish hair of the lady in the canvas, or might this have been a self-portrait? The artist was said to be from Deaconshire, and Henry spent a moment pondering whether he knew the location depicted. It certainly appeared inspired by the picturesque county, but while both the church and the hills harboured features that seemed familiar, he couldn't make a specific recollection.

As fascinating as the painting was, what truly inspired Henry was the artist herself. Whenever Henry visited a new town, he liked to frequent local galleries. They were nice places to visit, and he preferred more gentile establishments than rowdy taverns. It was in one of these galleries that he first learnt of a controversial artist from the area. The curator let slip that the artist was female but stressed that this wasn't his reason for barring her work from his shop. After that, he refused to say anymore.

Other curators in nearby towns were equally reticent to speak of Ms Rose, but this secrecy only intrigued Henry more. Upon learning of her "revelation" from wicked Satanist to devout Christian, his interest was piqued. From that point, he sought out her paintings, being told time and time again that no self-respecting shopkeeper would touch her work. Her Rose Petals were lost to private hands it seemed.

Most curators were sceptical of the rumours surrounding her redemption, deeming such a feat to be impossible—but wasn't that the miracle that this artwork represented? As a deeply pious man, Henry believed such miracles were indeed possible; thus, the artwork before him now was a miracle of God that he could touch. This artwork was akin to the Grotto of Massabielle in Lourdes or his very own Turin Shroud. In form, it was ordinary; but in terms of art, it was extraordinary.

Henry could not well hope to afford such a Wonder, but this strange means of leasing was an opportunity not the be missed. Mr. Hayes in the shop had not seemed too worried about the length of the loan. It had been easy to push Mr. Hayes to extend the period of the lease from two years to five. He felt he could've tried for more, but he did not wish to take advantage of a poor fellow who had very few customers.

As the carriage approached the village of Lordale, there was still brightness in the sky, but the fields, hills and houses were all dark. This settlement was so small there was no church or electricity or gas lamps. There was a small post office, but if you wanted to send a telegram, you had to travel to the nearby town of Ghyll. Several villagers, including Henry, would commute to the town for work in the week and then church on Sunday. It was only a few miles away, and Henry wished to remain in the peaceful home that his parents built. The house seemed to resonate with memories of them, keeping them alive somehow as if their souls were tied to the place.

Horse hooves crunched gravel, signalling their arrival. The dark silhouette of his home came into view. Henry reapplied the wrapping around his new prized possession as best he could. The oak frame was bulky and heavy, but the coachman kindly helped Henry carry it not just inside but up to his master bedroom. Being an only child, he had the luxury of a room as large as his parents, and the seat of power merely shifted across the landing on the tragic day when his last remaining parent passed away.

After thanking and tipping the coachman, Henry set about lighting candles and oil lamps before moving furnishings about. Such was his enthusiasm for this miracle of art, he wanted the canvas on the wall before bedtime. To wake on a holy day to such a piece would be most wonderful indeed.

Henry toiled for hours. There was no church bell to announce each hour, but steadily a bright moon rose outside. With only himself in a large house, Henry had grown used to the quiet. Odd noises, glances from figures in portraits and flickers of candlelight no longer bothered him, but it was nice to have a task to keep his mind occupied.

Lunar light crept into his bedroom and shimmered in the polished stone of the landing as it shone through a window across the other side of the house. It would be a couple of days until the moon was full, but such nights always reminded him of his youth. It had been a family tradition to do activities on full moon nights, such as playing games or walking through near-by fields. Even now, on nights like this, he might sense the presence of his parents about the house. These oc-currences didn't spook Henry as he believed it was sim-ply these recollections repeating in his mind. Memories were not unlike ghosts, he reasoned; in some way, his parents would always remain alive in his thoughts. And living in the house that they built, his memories—and thus, his parents—were much closer. It was a source of comfort for him.

Finally, the painting was up, and he'd rearranged furnishings and tidied the room too. Henry sat in his armchair and took a moment to relax and appreciate his labours. He glanced over at a grandfather clock by the door and was surprised to see the hour had passed midnight. Not wanting to cast the canvas in darkness so soon after mounting it, he kept an oil lamp on his bedside table alight and climbed into a four-poster bed. Rose Petal VI was framed, as intended, between the two posters at the foot of his bed. He lay there and regarded the artwork once more.

The painting represented a life that he sought, but he did not want to sell his parent's home. However, if his recent successes with his fledgling business continued, he may be able to afford a second home in such a location. The attractive young redhead looked upon him; the thought of such a beautiful wife warmed his soul. Sleep caught Henry with a smile etched on his face.

There came a loud, trembling sound not long after attaining sleep, and Henry awoke in a paroxysm of fright. Such a sound was never heard in this isolated country village, and yet it seemed incredibly close as if originating from a room in another corner of his house. Henry sat up and shivered, feeling an icy chill. The oil lamp at his bedside was still alight. With bleary eyes, Henry glanced around the room fearing something had fallen due to his rushed late-night labours. But paintings hung straight, wardrobe doors were closed, and the grandfather clock stood firm—nothing was out of place. The clockface told of the hour—one o'clock—but it had been years since it announced these milestones in time. No, the grand, old clock was very much mute, and Henry turned his gaze to the new painting beyond the end of his bed, where a church gleamed in painted moonlight. The sound that awoke

Henry had unmistakeably been a single chime of a church bell.

Henry spent a few moments recovering his composure, before cursing the vividness of his dream. All was silent now, except for the ticking of the clock. He felt foolish but relieved. Accepting that the sound was purely imagined, he snuffed out the oil lamp.

Henry turned over as the light in the room faded with the gradual dimming of the wick of the oil lamp. The painting by Magdalena Rose faded too, yet Henry had the strange notion that it faded more slowly. Momentarily, he felt that same icy chill run down his body towards the painting. There, the lady looked out innocently, but that sweet face... In the last moment before darkness came, it did not seem the same.

A PAINTING BY
MAGDALENA ROSE (III)

When Henry awoke in the morning, he regarded the woman in the painting. It was not quite the delight he had hoped. The curious event in the night had dampened the moment. He recalled times, particularly in his youth, when he'd imagined monsters in the shadows of mundane objects. Of course, it was just folded clothes hung over a chair or something similar, but in the middle of the night, the mind conjured such fancies. This, Henry told himself, was also why he saw the expression of the lady in the painting changed. But what of the chime? Every fibre in his body knew that was not dreamt. Could it be the grandfather clock remarkably tolling again? No. The sound emanated not from beside the door but from the wall opposite his bed, where the painting hung.

Henry took the horse-drawn omnibus with his fellow villagers to St Paul's in Ghyll. He'd planned to extol about his new purchase and invite them to see the miraculous artwork that proved Magdalena Rose's discovery of God, but now, he neglected to even mention it.

Henry sang the hymns in church with great vigour. God was righteous and glorious and would never fail to protect him. His little party from Lordale always sang the loudest; the townsfolk's hearts just weren't quite in it.

Henry's late parents had gossiped about an event in the year of his birth, 1880. Some terrible event led to fires in the street and wanton destruction within the grounds of the church, yet the cold light of day had sobered the townsfolk, who later feigned ignorance. The rumours were of an act of necromancy or bedevilled magic. It rather cast a shadow over the town and a mistrust in its people—another reason Henry preferred to remain in Lordale—but hadn't he rather lost his passion for his new purchase in the same way as the townsfolk's faith had gone adrift?

The thought irked Henry. He was being ridiculous. It was nothing more than a twinge of buyer's remorse coupled with the fact that some of his fellow villagers knew of Magdalena Rose, and he wasn't prepared for all the "satanist" comments that would come when he mentioned her name. Besides, this town was no place to approach such subjects.

Henry rallied in his resolve. After a week with the painting, such daft notions would be gone. Yes, he was sure. His passion would be renewed, and he would invite his fellow villagers to his house to view it then.

Returning home, Henry enjoyed a Sunday lunch and a sunny day toiling in his garden. He took special care when tending to the graves of his parents who were buried at the boundary of the property, where the garden met a woodland. His parents had not wanted to be buried at the cemetery in Ghyll due to the rumours of desecration that had taken place.

Henry's evening was mostly spent reading, but he couldn't concentrate. There was something he wanted—no, needed—to check. Returning to his master bedroom, he first glanced at the painting, and all was as it should be. He then opened the grandfather clock and inspected the mechanism. He got a swift answer to his enquires, the hammer that once caused the clock to toll was not there, removed years ago by his father no doubt.

A simple answer is always welcome even if it doesn't resolve a mystery, but he thought a moment on the fiction that he was reading. He enjoyed reading a Penny Dreadful now and then, and hadn't he read an article in a stiff broadsheet about how such uncouth and roguish publications were warping people's minds, especially the young and impressionable? Was this his answer? An overactive mind?

Henry moved to the painting and inspected it closely. Here were the brushstrokes guided by God's healing hand, and he couldn't resist tracing them with his finger. The woman's countenance was that of someone relaxed and content; in the night, he thought he'd seen her grin. What Henry felt, unsurprisingly, was paint on canvas, not fire on brimstone. His inspection served to put his mind at ease. There was nothing extraordinary materially, yet he still regarded the artwork as a miracle.

Afterwards, Henry went about his nightly routine and prepared for his work in the morning. He went up to bed much earlier than he had the previous night. Having snuffed out the oil lamp, Henry couldn't help but glance once more at the canvas. All was dark. There was no ghost light from the frame. All was well and sane.

A deep sleep caught Henry. A disruptive few days had taken a toll on him. He lay as he so often did, on his side facing the window. Being summer, just a single sheet lay across him. Dreams swirled to and fro, caught in the gentle breeze gifted by an open window.

Woodland creatures muttered outside and a scent of cut grass and straw wafted in. But the scent filling his nose grew thicker and staler. It muddied his dreams, then the stench became rancid. Deep chimes trembled aloud.

A fit of fright stole the beat of Henry's heart. With the first peal of the bell, he opened his eyes. There was a glow of moonlight about the room even though lunar rays never entered as the only window was north-facing. A cold breath brushed the nape of his neck and with it came a potent whiff of rotten flesh. An icy touch slipped between the bedsheet and his skin.

Momentarily, all was still, then came the second toll of a bell. Frosty fingers walked along his side and across his torso before pausing over his heart. Hairs on his chest stood on end, frozen rigid. A hand pressed against him.

The pressure on Henry's chest forced him to fight for a breath, as there came a third and final chime. An ice-cold body cuddled up to him, and the hand on his chest reached inside—it clasped his heart and squeezed tightly.

Henry was paralysed in terror. His heart did not beat, and his breath would not come. His eyes raced around, but he saw nothing. The metallic peal resounded in his ears, but then as it tailed off so did the vice-like grip of ice. As the echo waned, the cold clutch receded. Warmth came back to his chest and his heart restarted with a kick of adrenaline.

Henry's muscles jolted as blood flooded through them once more, and he rolled onto his back. Now he saw Magdalena's artwork aglow, now painted with moonlight that spilt into his bedroom. His eyes focused on the church. A daemonic entity clung to its sounding spire. Lights were on inside the chapel, and shadows passed by the windows. A new terror struck him. The whole scene was alive and scattered with hellish creatures that he could not resolve. Yet there was something worse than that—something was missing. The rose-haired woman was not in the frame.

As the third toll became a faint echo, the air shifted about him. It was maddening, like seeing heat haze in the night. And yet it lingered and swirled turbulently above him. Henry lay paralysed once more. The breathless breeze stirred and gently receded towards the painting. This distortion was like waves of refracted light with a will all their own. As it moved further away, Henry just barely resolved a recognisable form. The more it drifted towards the painting, the clearer it became. As the final trace of sound ebbed away, the distortion reached the artwork and dissolved.

There were to be no more chimes at this hour, but the new silence was not to last long. In the moment before, Henry's eyes locked with a woman who stood at the recently vacated spot in the painting. Wretched wrinkles ran across a face bubbling with boils, and her grubby clothes were torn and tatty and exposed a frail body with veins as stiff as bristles on a broomstick. On her face was etched a grimace that only a few stained teeth could grasp onto. The bright canvas slowly faded, as if a cloud were passing across the face of an out-of-frame moon. Original brushstrokes returned and the hag grew younger. When darkness finally came, so too did a scream that startled prey and predator alike in the woodland beyond the window and across the garden.

A PAINTING BY
MAGDALENA ROSE (IV)

H enry lay awake for the rest of the night, his
sheets drenched in sweat. Even if he could sleep,
he daren't. What if she came back? The worst thing of
all was not being able to see the hands of the grandfather clock. The bell tower in Magdalena's painting did
not chime every hour, but if it did, it would chime on
the hour. But without knowing the time, every minute
felt as though the next hour was just one minute away.
At any moment, she may return. But finally, the drapes
brightened as they held back the morning light, and the
bell hadn't tolled again.

When Henry finally resolved the hands of the grand, old clock at half past five, he allowed himself a moment to relax his tensed muscles, but daylight brought a new problem—he would be able to see the artwork if he looked over. What would be there? The pleasant disguise or the true madness of Magdalena's mind?

The painting had paralysed him in the night, and Henry felt that the gaze of the lady may trigger a repeat. He delayed a moment, summoning courage, but then, throwing off the clinging, damp sheet, he rose out of bed.

Henry marched to the canvas. He was unable to avoid a momentary glance, his curiosity was such. He saw what he expected, the cunning disguise. He ripped the painting down and leant it against the wall, turned away. This artwork was truly devilish. Magdalena was unable to get anyone to purchase her daemonic monstrosities, but by giving her wolves sheep's clothing in her Rose Petals, her daemons could feed.

Henry looked at the back of the heavy frame. He wanted to destroy it, but the frame was too firm for him to simply put a foot through it; he would need to fetch tools. The pressing need, though, was to get it to a place where the woman in the painting could no longer watch him.

The weight of the painting caused him to struggle. Sure, he'd had help bringing it up when he'd arrived, but in his excitement, he'd rather overlooked the weight, he judged. Henry's first triumph was getting the artwork out of his master bedroom and sealing the door shut behind him. With one bare foot under the frame, he lifted it and took a large stride forward. He wanted it out the way before the next hour came. Heavy stride by heavy stride, he got the painting to the top of his stone stairs.

He didn't want to destroy the painting, not yet anyway. A thought grew in the back of his mind. Something supernatural or daemonic lay within the object he was carrying. He surely felt the weight of it. But the canvas acted as some kind of seal holding it inside, only to be released on the stroke of an hour and only when the painted church chimed. If the canvas was torn, what would happen? Would the daemon be destroyed or set free?

Another thought crossed his mind, telling him that the church would not toll in daylight. Perhaps it was the moonlit setting or the fact that this creature seemed nocturnal, but he believed he had till dusk to decide upon a course of action. Henry took great pains to carry the painting down the twisting stairs, and then he cleared out a storage cupboard before carrying the painting inside. He stood it to face a dusty wall, then closed the cupboard behind him. Task accomplished,

Henry collapsed in a heap on a leather sofa and took heavy breaths spliced with both relief and fear.

The day grew brighter, and Henry remained firmly in the comfort of his sofa when he should have taken a carriage to his office in Ghyll. Carriages ran like omnibuses in the small village of Lordale, and if you either missed or hadn't made a booking, you likely wouldn't get another opportunity. Attending his office seemed unimportant today—he needed to recover—but he disliked that he had no way to inform his colleagues of his absence. It was a common courtesy, but without a post office in Lordale, he could not send a telegram. Henry then had a thought that made him wish that he hadn't missed his carriage.

As the artwork was leased, he couldn't afford to destroy it lest he'd need to pay Mr. Hayes an extortionate sum. However, if he were to return it to Mr. Hayes, he'd need to visit Ghyll to arrange a delivery.

Moments later, Henry saw his neighbour, Mr. Ernest Taylor, walking by. Mr. Taylor was an elderly gentleman whose grey hair was peeking out beneath his bowler hat. At church, he'd made mention of a doctor's appointment in Ghyll today, and seeing an opportunity, Henry rushed to his front door.

'Afternoon, Ernest,' Henry called out.

'I think you'll find it's still morning,' he shouted back from the edge of Henry's front lawn. 'What are you doing here and not at your office?'

'I had a dreadful night. I'm still a little out of sorts.'

'I can see that,' Ernest said, now walking down the gravel track towards Henry. 'You looked a bit peaky at church yesterday, come to think.'

'I'm on the mend now. Can I ask a favour?'

'You want me to tell your office that you're ill and not skiving.'

'I'd appreciate that, but I have another request.'

'Fire away, young man.'

'I need to send an item to a Mr. Hayes in Lyeminster,' Henry said. 'He's a charming fellow with some fine artworks.'

'I'd be happy to take your item to the post office in Ghyll,' Ernest offered.

'Hmm. I don't think that will work. It's a painting, you see, too cumbersome for a crowded carriage. No, could you ask a cabman to collect and transport it? I hate to be a burden, but I'd really appreciate it if it could be sent later today. Could you ask a cabman to visit me as soon as you arrive in Ghyll?'

'Oh. I'll do my best. You know how hard it can be to get a carriage without a prior reservation. Cabmen seem to be in such short supply what with so many choosing to be private chauffeurs. And who can blame them when they get twice the rate driving those new-fangled motor cars? Nevertheless, I shall endeavour to arrange your cab.'

'Thank you. Let me write down the address of his shop.' As Henry was writing the note, he added, 'Mr. Hayes pointed out his home address to me across from his shop. I'll make a note of that too as I expect it may arrive after hours.' Henry gave his neighbour the note and bid him a good day.

Henry paced to and fro for much of the afternoon. He remained close to his front window as he anxiously waited for a cab, but the hours passed and no carriages came. His wait was exacerbated by the determination of his mind to dwell upon the cursed painting. How could such a thing exist? What witchcraft was Magdalena Rose capable of? Where would the painting end up once he returned it?

The last question had been what troubled him to the point that he penned a letter to Mr. Hayes with a warning of the evil within the canvas. He tried his best to make such absurdities seem plausible enough so that his warning would be heeded. Henry's conscience was clearer having written the note, but he questioned where the painting had been before.

Surely, Mr. Hayes couldn't already be aware of its bedevilment. Could he? And what of those who had leased it prior? Had they experienced the curse and given a warning? Mr. Hayes would have to consider such things if it was reported on multiple, independent occasions.

The wrinkles of worry that etched across Henry's forehead deepened as he saw Ernest approaching his house.

Meeting him at his door, Ernest confirmed the fear festering within Henry's gut. There were no carriages available today. Ernest bemoaned the lack of cabmen once more, but he buoyantly recounted how he'd negotiated a cab that was both earlier and cheaper than originally offered by paying in advance. It would arrive tomorrow afternoon. Henry expressed his gratitude and paid him back whilst hiding his anxiety towards having the painting for another night.

'Something troubled me, though,' Ernest said. 'If you visit the office tomorrow, you won't be able to give the cabman the painting.'

'In such a case I will leave a note that it is in the outhouse. As you have already paid, it should be no trouble.'

'Ah, very well. May you feel better soon.' With that, Ernest left.

As troubled as Henry was to not be rid of the artwork, the thought of the outhouse provided some comfort—he could get it out of his house. Henry noted how the sun was already dropping low in the sky, so he wasted no time in moving the painting from the storeroom to the outhouse.

With the cursed artwork out of his home, he finally found relief was able to override his anxiety. Henry's worrying meant he hadn't eaten all day. Food gave him a boost of energy, but as the sky turned red with the setting sun, the fear of hearing church bells returned once more.

It was outside, he told himself. And it was out of sight, but the spectre of eight o'clock loomed over him. Henry tried to shake off the notion, then picked up a book and opened it at the bookmark. Black text on off-white pages was what he saw, but he didn't register the words. He may have been staring at the next page in his book, but nothing went in. While his eyes stared, his mind swirled. Glances to a timepiece on the mantel became more and more frequent as the minutes ticked to the hour.

When it finally came to eight o'clock, he kept his head firmly in his book. Dusk was heavy outside; the blood-red sky had drained out leaving only bluish-black. Henry's book glided in sweaty palms. He stared and stared without hearing a sound, and when he finally looked back to the clock, he breathed an audible sigh. The eight o'clock hour was passed.

A similar circus played out at nine o'clock; again, there were no phantom bells. Now, though, Henry found his head bobbing and his eyes closing. He'd had such little sleep, and he wasn't getting anything done. He resolved that the only course of action was to get an early night.

Henry was in bed before ten o'clock but waited with his oil lamp alight for the hour to pass; he anticipated needing a full hour to fall asleep despite his tiredness. In the place of Rose Petal VI was a family portrait photograph. He'd never wanted to move it from his parents' bedroom until now. The monochrome picture was unusual in many ways; his parents were creative and didn't want a stiff, formal portrait. Instead, this photograph was set in a wide format more typically associated with landscape images. His mother had a kind smile, and his father, wearing his distinct circular spectacles, was not looking out of the portrait but rather at a young Henry, whose fingers were playing with his mother's blonde curls. It was a comfort to sleep under the watch of kind, reliable faces instead of that bewitched woman. Nevertheless, Henry questioned whether he was out of earshot of the phantom tolls.

Ten o'clock passed, and after a brief sleep, he awoke before the eleventh hour. It passed too. Next was midnight. Henry recalled the trembling chimes and the ice-like grip that arrested his heart. The prospect of twelve tolls caused him to toss and turn. One chime stunned him; three had paralysed him; what would twelve bring?

There was no hope for sleep. All there was was fear and trepidation and angst. Henry thought of Magdalena. She was a miracle in the clutch of the devil. He thought of the grinning hag he'd seen fleetingly in the picture. This was her wish, to trick and torment men of God.

The grandfather clock ticked ever louder while Henry's sheets grew sticky with sweat. The oil lamp had burnt out, so he could not see the clock face. Midnight... Wasn't that the witching hour? Wasn't that when Magdalena would enact her truly evil deeds? Henry didn't know how close the hour was at hand, but there was no point checking if the hour had already passed. He was expecting to hear the chimes now. He grumbled that there was no cabman today, and he bemoaned that he'd not moved the painting further away from his property. How foolish he'd been to act with only a half measure. Still, Henry waited, all the while his grip on his sheets growing tighter.

And there it came—a trembling toll as if from a church bell just outside his window. He thought the whole village should hear it. The dread that it struck held a dead weight that pinned him to the bed. Paralysis once more seized his body. He lay on his back only moving his eyes from the window to the door. There was no extra light in the room, but he knew the artwork in the outhouse was aglow in its own moonlight. And the rose-haired lady was free to leave her boundary.

In the brief pause between chimes, there came a lilting sound from downstairs as if a woman was humming a tune. The next peal drowned it out, and by the time the second toll subsided, Henry heard the same playful tune, now from the top of the stairs. There was no creak or sound of footsteps, but Henry knew the woman had indeed vacated the confines of her painting. Henry's eyes turned towards the direction of the child-like song. As the next bell came, Henry postulated that the woman had this and nine more tolls till she would be drawn back to her painting.

A figure with matted, red hair covering her face and a grubby, torn gown emerged at the edge of his vision by the door. She was aglow as if in the light of a full moon. She stepped past where he could see clearly, then he felt someone enter his bed without moving the sheets. In the next pause, he both heard and felt a breath at the nape of his neck. The rancid foetor returned.

An icy hand froze beads of sweat on his chest and came to rest above his heart. The hand pressed firmly. It sunk into him, chilling his blood. Dry, ropey hair floated across Henry's face. The toothless grinning hag gazed down at him as she clasped her icy hand like a vice on his heart. Henry lay frozen gazing at the hag as the bells struck. Each one stilled a beat of his heart as frost threatened to bite.

Henry's consciousness was slipping. Now he saw multiple figures above him. It didn't seem to be blurred vision as one of the new ghostly apparitions was that of a man wearing circular glasses. The other was a young, attractive woman with curly hair. His final glimpse before passing out implied that these two spectres were fighting to pull the hag off him.

A PAINTING BY MAGDALENA ROSE (V)

I t was late when there came a knock at the door of Mr. & Mrs. Hayes' home. Mr. Hayes was attending to some accounts. The numbers that were loose in his head would be lost if he got up from the dining room table. But at another impatient rap of the doorknob, Mr. Hayes finally got up, grumbling.

'I'll get it, shall I?' Mr. Hayes shouted to his wife, but he got no answer. She was simply out of earshot, he judged. It was not uncommon in this house. Mr. Hayes went down a flight of stairs and met a cabman at his front door.

'Mr. Hayes?' the cabman asked. 'I have a delivery for your shop. It's in the cab.'

'At this hour?' Mr. Hayes checked his pocket watch. It was nearly eight o'clock.

'Took me a while to find you, sir. The instructions were a little vague, and I didn't collect the package till late afternoon.'

'Oh, very well,' Mr. Hayes said irritably. 'Would you mind leaving it the hall and closing the door on your way out? I need to get my work completed for the morning.'

The cabman agreed, and Mr. Hayes walked back up the stairs. He tried to gather the numbers that had been in his head, but as he feared, they were gone. Mr. Hayes sat at the dining table and followed the sound of the cabman's heavy boots clapping on his stone floor, then there came a loud thud as he set down a heavy item. Mr. Hayes wondered briefly what it might be, but getting the accounts completed was a more pressing matter.

Bells tolled around Lyeminster at eight o'clock and then nine o'clock. All was quiet in the house. Mr. Hayes expected that his wife would come up to offer him supper close to ten o'clock. He'd busily worked away in the hope that he may be finished by that time, but it was likely to take a little longer. As expected, he heard Doris closing doors between the kitchen and the lounge, and then moving from the lounge to the hallway. There was an audible gasp, and Mr. Hayes realised that she must've been surprised by the package.

Church bells chimed throughout the town. Being in the centre it was always a noisy affair, and Mr. Hayes seldom went to bed before midnight as the chorus would only wake him. Yet this time, the metallic peals startled him. So familiar was Mr. Hayes with the churches and their timings that he could pick out each one. And yet, there now seemed a newer, closer one—so close that each chime vibrated his whole being. Ten booming clangs in amongst all the others.

When they finally stopped, he had to catch his breath. There were old churches that no longer sounded. 'Why do they need another bell?' Mr. Hayes grumbled aloud to the fresh silence. He expected a reply from his wife, but none came.

Mr. Hayes finished his sums, then wondered why Doris hadn't come upstairs yet. Was she inspecting the item that had been delivered? What could it be? It had sounded heavy, and it evidently surprised her. Might one of his art or antique dealers have sent some strange artefact his way? It wouldn't be the first time. It was always exciting to receive such strange packages. Mr. Hayes was reminded that this was how the painting by Magdalena Rose had come into his possession.

A thought occurred to Mr. Hayes, and valleys stretched down his forehead. Could it be...? Had he not pointed out his home address to that young man who'd leased that painting? Surely not. 'Doris?' he called out. There was no reply. He thought more on the artwork. There was something about it that he knew he hadn't witnessed. He'd close the shop a few minutes past five o'clock and was always home by six o'clock. It was a new routine, partly implemented due to his unease of being alone with Magdalena's painting after dark. As such, he'd never had to witness whatever phenomena it was that could cause an artefact with a five-year lease to return in five days. 'Doris?' he called out at much higher volume. Silence.

'No!' Mr. Hayes cried. 'You fool!' he shouted at himself. His chair scraped as he shot up from his desk. 'Doris, darling? Are you all right?' Nothing.

Mr. Hayes hurried to the stairs, papers falling to the floor in his haste. 'Doris, darling?' he repeated as he raced down the stairs. Without a response, his cry grew frantic, and darting into the hallway, he let out a harrowing shriek.

Doris Hayes lay lifeless on the hard polished floor. Mr. Hayes, in a wild frenzy, shook her, kissed her, and shouted at her—anything that might bring her back. As he held her, he felt a bite of frost on her skin. Her clothes were unmarked, but her chest was icy cold, with a pale blue-grey patch of skin close to her heart.

Mr. Hayes bawled aloud. Tears filling his eyes, he looked up, praying for a miracle. Then he saw it. There, propped against the wall, was the painting by Magdalena Rose, number six. Mr. Hayes held his dead wife and sobbed.

As Mr. Hayes cradled Doris' body, he rocked backwards and forwards, screaming at himself and the artwork. After a while, there came a little tinkle from the lounge. A quaint little clock with small garden birds on chirped happily. Mr. Hayes watched it through the open door. It was always first to mark the hour, purposely a minute fast so the town's bells didn't give them a start. As the colourfully painted birds chirped their last before eleven o'clock, the bells all around the town began their hourly argument once more.

Mr. Hayes turned his head slowly towards the artwork. His body prickled as the new bell tolled once more. First, he saw the contented expression of the young, rose-haired woman, before noticing a brightening candlelight glow from inside the church behind her. Then, as if the moon in this painted world emerged from behind the clouds, the whole canvas gleamed with lunar light. Some hideous outline seemed to cling to the church's spire, visible only now. Other hellish creatures emerged from shadowy crevices and soon the whole canvas was infested. And then he saw again the young, contented lady. Except she was neither young nor contented, but an old hag with a gummy smirk. And her eyes locked with his as she stepped out from the painting.

Author Note

I wish to thank you for reading my anthology of seasonal ghost stories. My writing journey started seven years ago with a desire to build and explore a county steeped in mystery, folklore and eerie intrigue. As I crafted my gothic county of Deaconshire—inspired by the beauty and isolation of the UK's Lake District—many story ideas emerged. This anthology collects some of the ghost stories, and I opted to use different periods and seasons to afford each tale a unique feel.

If you enjoyed these short stories, you may also like my debut novel, Beneath The Chimes—a Victorian ghost story that journeys deep into this county's dark, mysterious heart. It is my odyssey of horror, my ode to gothic fiction. Available now on Amazon.

Connecting with a reader audience is my most valued goal, but as a self-published author, I rely on the support of readers like you. If you enjoyed these stories, leaving a review online is the best way to help others discover them. N. P.

Acknowledgements

I dedicate this book to my Grandma Joyce, a strong and resilient woman whose advice I still heed. She'd always encourage seeing something through to completion. She might have found my stories a little strange, but she helped instil persistence and determination in me that has seen these stories published. And she might have liked that the music from her childhood features prominently in The Dream House.

My parents and brother continue to be a huge source of support and encouragement, which I always value.

I harbour special thanks to a lifelong friend, Adam Pritchett. You've read all these stories, shared invaluable feedback, and lent your voice to my promotional material. All being well, you'll also bring these characters to life in the audiobook. I really appreciate it.

I thank everyone who read these stories whilst they were rough drafts. Stephen Hegarty, I always value your insightful thoughts. Dave & Elaine Chant, I continue to be very grateful for your guidance on story flow and English grammar knowledge. Ryan Broomfield, your enthusiasm to read my tales keeps me motivated.

To the Brighter Writers group in Lytham, your encouragement has been exceptional. Writing The Dream House was particularly enjoyable because you listened to the chapter drafts within days of me writing them. To have an audience keen to know how things play out (even when I'm asking the same questions) was great motivation to continue.

I also extend thanks to Dr Stephen Carver for his manuscript critique and subsequent edit. To find an editor who loves gothic fiction and "gets" what I'm striving for has been invaluable.

Finally, I would like to share my gratitude to the fantastic artists who've contributed towards this publication: my cover artist, Fay Lane; my map designer, Dewi Hargreaves; my chapter heading illustrator, Lindsay Baang; and the visual artist behind my promotional material, Iulian Gutu. Your artwork and skill are the flourishes that I could not give.

About the author

N. P. Arrowsmith is an author of adult horror fiction and a Chartered Engineer with the Royal Aeronautical Society. He lives in Turin, Italy; however, the inspiration for his fictional county of Deaconshire was formed whilst hiking around The Lake District, UK.

Also by N. P. Arrowsmith

BENEATH THE CHIMES

An Odyssey of Horror
An Ode to Gothic Fiction

Available NOW on Amazon

Printed in Dunstable, United Kingdom